Fifty Reasons to Say "Goodbye"

A Novel by Nick Alexander

ISBN: 2-9524899-0-4

Nick Alexander

Nick Alexander was born in 1964 in the U.K. He has travelled widely and has lived and worked both in the U.K. and the U.S.A. He currently lives with two cats and three goldfish in France. *Fifty Reasons to Say, "Goodbye"* was Nick's first novel. The sequels, *Sottopassaggio, Good Thing, Bad Thing,* and *Better Than Easy* are also available from BIGfib Books as is the standalone novel and short story collection, *13:55 Eastern Standard Time.* For more information, to contact the author, or to order extra copies please visit his website on www.nick-alexander.com

Acknowledgements

Thanks to Fay Weldon and Robert Thicknesse for encouraging me when it most counted. Thanks to my friends and family for their support. Thanks to everyone who has filled my life with these stories and to everyone who shared with me when I occasionally ran out of material of my own. Thanks to my mother for giving me my first dictionary and to Matthew for giving me the first novel that ever caught my interest. Thanks to Apple computer for making such wonderful reliable work tools, and to BIGfib Books for making this physical book a reality.

"Each time the losses and deceptions of life teach us about impermanence, they bring us closer to the truth. When you fall from a great height, there is only one possible place to land; on the ground, the ground of truth. And if you have the understanding that comes from spiritual practice, then falling is in no way a disaster, but the discovery of an inner refuge."

- Sogyal Rinpoche

"Like a roller in the ocean, life is motion, move on. Like a wind that's always blowing, life is flowing, move on."

- Abba

Prologue

My father was born in the top floor bedroom of his parents' guesthouse, the mysteriously named "Donnybrook" – my grandmother told me all about it. It overlooked the beach, and on the cold stormy November night he was born, the rain lashed against the rattling sash windows. Between bouts of searing pain she glimpsed the raging sea, wondering if this was in some way not-meant-to-be; she was always looking for signs.

But as soon as he was born, the storm moved on and she dozed exhaustedly watching the sunrise, listening to the screaming laughter of the seagulls on the roof, the baby sleeping in her arms. She knew that everything would be OK after all.

Dad said his only childhood memories were of the beach. Long, endless summers of buckets and spades and adopted aunties, of gritty sandy sandwiches and cold, deep, wet burials by adopted brothers. Of dribbling chocolate flaked ice creams and sandy dams failing, crumbling against the incoming tide. As an adult he would forever wonder what city kids did all summer long.

It was on the beach he met his wife, my mother, not a mile away from Donnybrook. She was a Londoner on summer holiday alone; her parents were working. She looked like Rita Hayworth. Sometimes she laughed easily, sometimes she stared icily at the sea; he was intrigued. They slept together twice, she got pregnant, they got married.

His first girlfriend was heartbroken; she married the best man instead.

The baby died at birth; apparently Mum nearly died too. The war stopped them trying again for seven years.

Dad told me that in the drifting stifling sands of North Africa, he had thought of the beach all the time, a taunting symbol of a carefree past. That's why when he returned he wanted to live there again, that's why they moved into his parents' house.

He said that the war had changed him, that the sadness of it all had softened him. My mother had changed too – she'd been hardened by rationing and air raid shelters.

They had a child every three years, regular as clockwork for as long as it was possible. I ended up the last of four.

Dad's parents died only three years apart. They finished their lives in the top rear bedroom, his old room, with only the railway station to look at.

The sea view rooms were saved illogically for absent but ever-imminent paying guests, but people no longer went to Eastbourne on holiday, preferring exotic sands with foreign names.

Eventually they bought carpet for all of our rooms, mine was orange – it was the seventies. When the wind blew off the sea, the carpet lifted as the air pushed through the floorboards.

Our house slowly passed from being a screaming nursery school to a bubbling cauldron of adolescent and menopausal angst.

Of course, we were fine; we were busy being adolescents. We just reacted to Mum's hysteria and Dad's sulking by shouting even louder. We hated everyone anyway – society, grown-ups, each other; our parents were just part of the décor. But for them, it was hard, Mum spent a third of her time in bed with an endless series of mysterious illnesses, Dad spent the evenings walking along the beach, looking for calm and refuge.

During the endless summers they would pack us off with picnic, buckets, windbreaks. They would stay behind to do the adult things, the shopping, the repairing, the decorating, and the arguing. I think they envied us, with our friends and our games and our laughter.

Mum came to resent Dad's friends. I don't know how that happened, but one by one she found a reason to dislike them and slowly, one by one, they stopped coming. She never seemed to laugh anymore. I guess that was when he started to doubt.

One by one my brothers left, for wives or distant jobs or college.

One summer, sitting on a green, seaweed encrusted wall, with his feet dangling in the water, Dad admitted that he didn't love her anymore. Three summers later on the same wall he decided to leave. He told me first. I felt sad, abandoned, but honoured to be the first to know.

When he told her, I was watching from the back garden. The window was open and by holding my breath I could hear. She stared out of the front window.

She said, "Well, whatever you want. I mean, why would anyone else matter. It's always been all about you."

She said, "I want the house, and if you're dumping Mark on me, enough for us to live on. Hopefully he'll be leaving soon enough anyway."

She said, "And I want you to leave right now."

When they said goodbye it seemed very formal, very correct, very businesslike.

Dad moved out into a flat; it looked out over a tiny backyard with a broken motorbike in it.

Every weekend he would walk to the beach. Sometimes he would spend the day with me.

When she was there he would watch from a distance. If I saw him first I would wander casually down to the beachfront, escape so that we could spend the time together. He would sneak me into a pub, buy me a beer – I was sixteen. When they met she smiled tightly. There was never any drama.

I moved out only six months later, escaped to a rented room in a friend's house – Mum's new regime was all the motivation I needed; it felt like rationing was back.

I worked for a few years, studied enough to get the exams I had dropped out on, and then went to college. Sometimes I used to visit her, but she always seemed bitter, always depressed.

She ended up all alone in the big house and complained about it, said it was too big – as though it had been imposed on her. I used to come down to see Dad too. I don't know why but he never visited me once in Manchester.

At night we would sit on the concrete steps leading down to the beach, now littered with indestructible McDonalds' boxes. Mostly he was happy, but sometimes, without explanation he would weep.

Sometimes we saw Mum gazing from the window, just before she closed the curtains.

Dad always asked, "How's your mother?"

I always replied, "Oh, you know, the same."

I'm sure she saw us, but she never made any sign.

He died while I was at college. He was with his girlfriend.

Big surprise! No one knew.

She was at the funeral too, a thin woman with wild red hair. She wept hysterically. Our mother went home the second the service had finished. Strangely, we, the brothers, went to a pub. Guiltily we got drunk, laughed, had fun.

I think that that was when we realised that without our parents we got along just fine. It was our first ever get-together without them, it felt illicit and strangely relaxed.

The funeral was the last time the whole family was together in the same room. Reunited to say goodbye, – goodbye to our father, and then one by one to each other.

French Films

Jenny is lovely. She has a set of keys to our house. She used to go out with John, my flatmate – she had a set of keys in those days too, probably the same ones. My big double bed catches the afternoon sun. Some days, when I come home she's asleep in the sun with my cat Sizzler.

We spend so much time together. We have our favourite coffee shop, our favourite pub.

She doesn't have a car, can't get to the out of town stores, so I take her on Saturdays – people are always assuming... I don't really know why we're *not* together. She probably doesn't fancy me, she goes for swarthy Italian types, although it has to be said that John is neither swarthy nor Italian.

He kissed me once, as we crossed on the stairs. I think he was drunk. No one knows about that, not even Jenny. I don't tell anyone. It was quite nice, a bit of a surprise really, but nice. Still we're very close.

I only had three girlfriends while I was at college. The first one slapped me the first time we kissed. It was apparently because I got a hard-on; I suppose she wasn't ready. The second was beautiful, Spanish. Her ex-boyfriend hit me over the head with a crowbar. I hadn't even slept with her and I'm not even sure that I wanted to, but I was in love with her. She used to make me laugh and I used to walk across town to see her. I used to go to sleep thinking about her. For some reason she didn't want to see me after that, as though it was my fault!

The last one, Rachel, used to help me mend my motorbike. My friend Andy always said that Rachel was a dyke; many years later he turned out to be right. We used to share a bed, Rachel and I, cuddle up when it was cold, but we never had sex. Some say we snogged at a party once, but I truthfully don't remember – too drunk. Andy, who was studying psychology, used to say that it was a classic case of justified memory-repression syndrome.

I suppose it's not a lot for twenty-three, perhaps it should worry me. But my social life since I moved to Cambridge is so full on, and Jenny fulfils most of my emotional needs.

She's here tonight; we've been watching television together. She's snuggled up to me on the sofa to watch a French film, *Betty Blue* – typical French, basically an arty excuse for a shag-fest. I'm worried that

Jenny will move her elbow, discover my hard-on. Being a man is like walking around with a shag/don't shag sign in your trousers.

"He's so cute," she says.

"Yes, well neither of them are exactly ugly," I reply.

"The French," says Jenny. "Makes you sick."

I shrug. "Not the French, just films. They don't have ugly people in films."

"Or even normal people," says Jenny. "She's sexy too. We try, the English, to look like that. But it's just pointless."

I laugh. "You're exaggerating. Beatrice Dalle isn't *that* pretty. She's sexy, dirty, but she's pretty vulgar too. You're prettier."

Jenny laughs. She fidgets, changes her position.

"Oh my God! Mark!" she exclaims. "Hard-on!"

A wave of red sweeps across my face. Lucky the lights are low.

"Sorry," I say. "The film. Too much shagging."

Jenny looks into my eyes.

I feel slightly sick. Embarrassment probably.

"It's OK," she says.

I fidget. I wish she'd move out of my face.

She kisses me. I am surprised – like *really* surprised. I don't react at all.

She says, "Make an effort." She tries again.

I try to make an effort but my stomach is churning.

Jenny stands. I think, *"Thank God!"* But she leads me to the bedroom next door.

"It's time," she says. "Enough pussying around."

I feel frozen, remote. A sort of *does not compute* feeling. I didn't know that we *had* been pussying around. I thought we were watching T.V.

She pushes me onto the bed, undoes my jeans, and climbs on top of me. She doesn't seem phased by the fact that I'm not really participating. She pulls off her top – she isn't wearing a bra. She grabs my head, pushes me down, down between the mother-warmth of her breasts, down over her stomach, down, down to the forest.

I'm doing my best but it's making me heave. I've never much liked all of that, down there; never could get off on those pictures of women with their ankles behind their ears.

She touches me, realises. "You have a puncture sir," she says. "That car's going nowhere."

I am offended.

"Don't worry," she says. "It'll come back."

It germs as just an idea of anger, of outrage at myself. The decision to let it happen is quite conscious, calculated, a way out. "This always fucking happens," I spit – a lie, for who could say? Too few opportunities to know.

11

I get up, pull on my chinos, and wriggle into a pullover.

"Mark, where are you going?"

I pull on my shoes. "Oh, fuck off!" I shout as I run out into the street. I wish I'd brought a raincoat.

I jog to the end of the road. I feel bad, but relieved. I'm shaking.

I crouch in the entrance to an alleyway and watch the rain spin past the orange streetlights. I have cigarettes in the pocket of my jeans. I blow the smoke behind me into the darkness until, eventually, I see her leave the house and go home.

The next day she comes to see me. "We need to talk," she says.

She says many things. She says that I am a selfish bastard, that she was worried all night. She's right, but there are things that are instinctive, things that you can't help but do – things that you can't explain, not even to yourself.

"Have you ever thought that you might be, well, gay?" she asks.

I say bad things. I say, "So anyone who doesn't like the smell of your vagina is gay, right?"

She shouts, she cries, she leaves.

I'm upset, but I'm glad.

Later on the phone, she says, "I think we should stop seeing each other."

I say, "I wasn't aware that we *were* seeing each other."

Later still, much later, we'll be friends again. I'll apologise to her, thank her even, for making me realise. But it will take a while.

A Loving Relationship

I start seeing Catherine six months after I split up with Jenny. Every night is insomnia night. Friends say things like, "Just use the extra time to read or something." My eyes are too tired to focus on the page, but still sleep eludes me until four a.m.

I lie awake, watch the headlights sweep the ceiling. I can't work out why, a feeling of unease, a tightness in the stomach.

Catherine's OK, I suppose. I expected her to be much more involved. She never seems to say much, other than, "Umm," and "I see," and "How do you feel about that?" It annoys me – if I knew how I felt then I wouldn't be seeing her.

"Why does that question annoy you so much?" Catherine asks.

It takes five visits for me to get to the point, because I don't know what the point is. I suppose that's what therapy is all about.

"Why do you think your girlfriend's suggestion that you might be a homosexual upsets you so much?" she asks.

I had said, "gay." Jenny had said, "gay." Catherine is paraphrasing.

A week later and we're having the same conversation, only this time I shrug. I say, "Maybe she's right."

Catherine laughs. It's the first time she has reacted to anything I have said.

"What?" I ask. I missed the joke.

"Walk into any gay bar and you'd know!" she says.

"Know what?"

She laughs again. "That you're not a homosexual."

On the way home I walk past The Burleigh Arms. John has told me it's gay. He knows from his days visiting every pub in Cambridge with the Sixty-Two Pub Club. It was the last one they tried, number sixty-two.

I peer through the windows; it looks like any other pub.

Wednesday evening, I go for a stroll, walk past it again.
Two men go in, laughing.

Thursday night, I open the door and walk in. It is the scariest thing I have ever done.

I stand for half a minute looking around the place, try to suppress the trembling in my hands. I lean against a wall – it feels awkward, uncomfortable, as though it's not my body.

"Maybe that's what Catherine meant," I think.

A man in the corner smiles at me – a round warm face, a good smile.

I leave. Outside I gasp. I had stopped breathing – stress does that to me.

"Look," says Catherine at my next visit. "You are *not* a homosexual."

I wonder why she says, "A homosexual," instead of just, "homosexual," or even, "gay." It sounds like a grammatical error, but I was never very good with grammar.

"Now tell me about this..." She glances at her notes. "Jenny, your *"friend.""* She lifts her fingers to form the speech marks.

On the way home I go back to the pub. I order a drink; I am trembling again. The man with the smile is there.

"Hello," he says.

His name is Nick. He has brown eyes and gappy teeth. He smiles a lot. We drink our pints, I tell him the story.

He says, "It's hard coming out."

"Is that what I'm doing?" I wonder.

I like talking to Nick better than Catherine. He seems to have more common sense. He hates shrinks.

Saturday, we meet in the park. We walk; we talk. He tells me about his family. His boyfriend is a fireman.

"He's very sexy in his uniform," he confides.

Monday night, and I'm back with Catherine, supposedly my fix after the weekend. Gone is the cool detachment of our previous meetings.

"Why did you go there?" she wants to know.

"You said that if I went to a bar, I would know," I reply.

"I doubt that I said that," she says.

I frown. I shrug. "You did."

She smiles. "Well if that's what you think you heard," she says. "Anyway," she sighs. "Do tell me about your "gay" night out." She makes the speech marks again.

I want to ask her what the " " is all about but I don't dare. I say, "It's OK really. It's just a pub."

"Did you talk to anyone?"

I nod. "Yeah, a man called Nick – nice, he has a boyfriend, a fireman."

Catherine closes her eyes, breathes deeply. She looks as if she's doing yoga. I fidget in my seat. I watch her.

"Look, Mark. You have to stop this before you do yourself harm," she finally says.

I feel strange, caught between tears and anger. I don't know why.

"Can I leave?" I gather my jacket towards me.

She looks at her watch. "In ten minutes," she says. "In the meantime, tell me about... whatever his name is."

I'm surprised. It is the first time she has ever forgotten a name.

"Nick?" I ask.

She nods.

I sigh. "I told you. He's nice."

"Are you, *attracted* to him?"

I frown. "In what way?"

"Well I'm not talking about his *intellect* now am I?!"

"What?" I feel angry but I'm still not quite sure why. "Do I *fancy* him?"

Catherine seems to swell, to sweat; her eyes burn. "Listen, Mark," she says. "I'm going to stop this conversation right now; it's not... good."

I stare at her.

"The only question you need to ask yourself is this, Mark: do you ever want to be in a long term, loving relationship?"

I smile incredulously. "Well, of course."

"Then, my dear Mark, you are *not* a homosexual." She smiles again.

I wrinkle my nose and open my mouth. "Sorry?" I say.

"Homosexuals don't *have* loving relationships," she says.

My mouth drops.

She shakes her head. "They have sex, Mark. Sex in bars, sex in back streets, sex in toilets. Now if that's what you want..."

In my mind I tell her to fuck off. In my mind I say, *"If you are a heterosexual then I'd rather be gay."* But for some reason I'm scared of her.

I say, "Oh dear, times up. See you next week then."

I am unimaginably angry. I lean against a wall outside until I can breathe properly.

I never return. I go to the Burleigh instead.

Sometimes I wonder if she did it on purpose, if she said it to push me. But my guess is that she just doesn't like gays.

A Beautiful Tart

From that moment on, my virginity is a weight I drag along behind me. It is something I need to get rid of. I tell Nick this, he understands. "Once I had decided, I slept with the first guy that came along. He wasn't even cute," he says.

I need to sleep with a man. I need to know, need to be sure.

It only takes a week of hanging around in the Burleigh for the opportunity to appear. His name is Andrew. He's beautiful – dark skin, high cheekbones, a sort of male Naomi Campbell. Only he's not a model, he's a postman. I like that idea.

At night he seemingly lives in the Burleigh. I tell Nick that I think he's beautiful.

Nick says, "Yeah. I spoke to him once. He's very lovely, very intelligent – a very beautiful tart. But you could do worse, for a first time."

The next evening I see him there with some friends. He smiles at me. I am behaving like an adolescent schoolgirl. "He smiled at me!" I tell Nick.

He sighs. "Go and say *hi* then."

I shrug. "Nah, he probably doesn't fancy me anyway," I say.

Friday, he's there again. This time he offers me a drink and then invites me back to his house for coffee. We both know what coffee means and we both want it; I am terrified.

Nick slips a condom into my hand as he pushes me towards the door. "Good luck," he says raising an eyebrow. "Don't worry."

Trembling, I walk back with him. His voice is smooth and calm.

I am scared. Scared of looking stupid, scared of not knowing what to do, scared of AIDS, scared of negotiating safe sex.

He sits me on the sofa and makes coffee. On the wall he has a safe sex poster. It shows a man holding a condom. It says, "Live to fuck, again and again."

"That's one thing I don't need to worry about then," I think.

He serves coffee on the little wooden table. My hand is trembling, the teaspoon rattles against the cup.

Andrew looks at me. "Are you OK?" he asks.

I smile at him. "Yeah, I erh…"

I am about to say that I have never done this before, but it suddenly strikes me as presumptuous. This could just be coffee after all.

He nods in an understanding way. He says, "I know."

I wonder what he knows and how. I wrinkle my brow at him.

He says, "I know what will help."

I cough. "Yes?" I say.

He says, "Put down your coffee cup."

I place it on the table; it clatters against the saucer as it makes contact. Andrew places one hand behind my head, kisses me on the lips. He pauses, looks into my eyes. I launch into him, years of unacknowledged desire welling up in me, driving me forwards. I kiss him madly, maniacally, a man deranged.

He says, "Hey, HEY! Calm down!" He laughs.

We lie on the sofa and hug and kiss. He slows me down. It is softer, more romantic than I imagined. It is more wonderful, more magical than I thought possible.

He pulls away. "Better?" he asks.

I nod. I have stopped trembling.

"Good," he says leading me to the bedroom.

The sex is soft. Bodies rub together. We caress and fondle each other to a slow climax.

I am expecting to leave, expecting even to be thrown out, but we lie and talk and eventually fall asleep in each other's arms. I feel more relaxed than I ever remember being.

When I wake up in the morning Andrew is already up. I wonder for a moment if this can last, if I have read him wrong, but then he appears in the doorway, smiling broadly.

"Get up, get out," he says laughing. "The job's done and I've got a life to live."

I frown at him.

"Oh and say hi to Nick for me!" he says with a wink.

I walk away from the house feeling complex and irrevocably changed.

I feel bigger, older, clearer – calm, relaxed and sad all at once.

Dork

It's been a dull day. Everyone has gone away for the weekend, well except for Nick and myself that is. He's already in the pub when I call, so I join him there. The sun is setting; the rays are forcing themselves through the dirt-frosted windows. The Burleigh can actually look OK at night, when the coloured lights disguise the tobacco stained walls, when cute bottoms are hiding the split seats, but at five p.m. empty, the place looks dreadful.

Nick tells me about his trip to New York, tells me misty-eyed of twenty bars, all ten times bigger than this place, all decorated in post-industrial, minimalist chic; all of them stuffed with beautiful gym bunnies with huge white teeth.

"Still something empty about the whole thing though," he says.

"Empty?"

"Something sterile, like everyone's smiling, *looking* like they're having fun."

"Sounds OK to me," I say with a shrug.

"Yeah." Nick shakes his head from side to side, thinking about it. "But somehow," he continues, "it seems as though they're just looking like they're having fun, instead of actually *having* any fun. Does that make any sense at all?"

I nod. "I suppose so; still got to be better than this though." I gesture around the room.

Only one other person is in the bar, sat at the far end of the lounge. He looks our age, twenty to twenty-five years old; he's tall, very thin, blond. He has the most horizontal eyebrows I have ever seen – they make him look very serious. He's writing postcards.

Nick sees me looking at him and glances over his shoulder. He leans in conspiratorially. The music, a dreadful instrumental version of the Carpenters' greatest hits, is thankfully turned down low. "Do you like him?"

I shrug. "No, not really my type."

Nick glances again. "Why not?"

"Don't know," I reply. "Maybe it's the fact that I like them short and dark, and he's tall and blond."

Nick nods.

"Maybe it's because he's filling in postcards."

Nick frowns.

"So he's a tourist."

"So?"

"A heartbreaker."

Nick smiles and nods.

"Or maybe it's just because he looks about as skinny and serious and dorky as anyone I've ever seen."

"OK, OK!" Nick waves at me to stop. He pulls a cigarette from his packet of Marlboro, offers me one.

"Only trying to help," he says lighting up both of our cigarettes.

I glance over at the guy again. He's chewing his biro, looking into the middle distance. He smiles at me, flashing big white teeth.

Nick looks over his shoulder again; the guy looks back at his postcard.

"So actually it's *you* that likes him," I tease.

Nick shrugs. "Well yes actually," he replies. "But I've got, well you know, the B problem."

I cross my eyes and stick my tongue out. "The B problem?" I ask.

"Boyfriend."

I laugh. "It's not supposed to be a problem Nick. It's supposed to be The Solution."

Nick glances at the man again; he looks up from his postcard and nods a half *hello* to him.

Nick gets up. "Sorry, I can't help myself," he says to me, crossing the bar.

I can hear their voices, Nick's, and an American accent, but not the words. I flick through a free magazine and when I glance over Nick beckons to me.

The man smiles broadly and shakes my hand. "Dirk," he says. His accent is indeed American. His voice is broad and deep, rich and smooth.

"Nice voice," I think.

He shakes my hand. His hands are huge and slim – the image of his body – and his grasp is firm. Nick chats to him maniacally, as though he's running out of time.

"Of course..." I realise, *"he is! Darren will be here soon."*

I watch them talk. I feel unusually calm, reflective. I am thinking about myself, here, now, and the effect of his presence on me. I am surprised at the instant attraction I feel, despite all I have said about him not being *my type*.

It seems to be entirely because of his voice, because I like the slow deliberate way he constructs his phrases, because I like the vibrations the sound waves seem to make in my chest.

He's answering Nick but looking at me, questioningly. He's a student, he explains, on exchange to Cambridge. He's studying philosophy. "Only for a year," he says.

I interrupt the chat by asking him the million-dollar question. "Why?"

"I'm sorry?" he asks.

"Why philosophy?"

There is a pause. Nick wrinkles up his nose as if it's the most stupid question he has ever heard. Dirk looks at me, a half smile on his lips. His eyes shine.

"Why?" he laughs. "Well," he pauses, weighing up each word. "I suppose the reason is to gain some insight, however... lightweight, into the big *Why*. The why are we here? The why does it all seem so pointless?" His voice hesitates almost inaudibly as he says, "pointless."

I look at him intently. I wonder about that sadness.

"Well good. A worthy cause if ever there was one," interjects Nick. "Any insights so far?"

I sigh and look at him. Dirk pulls his eyes away from mine. He doesn't just look away – I can feel him pull them away, breaking contact, reluctantly.

His voice is upbeat, less serious. "Sure, I guess only corny stuff, but, well I suppose the more I think about life, the more it seems that it's just about, well, erm..."

"Sex?" asks Nick. "Well you don't need a degree in philosophy to know that!" he laughs.

"Love," says Dirk. "Actually I think it's love. In its many forms."

"Oh," says Nick.

"Strange concept I know, Nick." I open my eyes wide; wriggle my brow at him. "But one could actually link those two concepts: sex and love."

The door to the bar pushes open and Darren appears.

"Talking of which," laughs Nick, pushing himself out of his seat.

"I'm parked on double yellows, can we go?" says Darren, nodding a *hi* to me.

Nick mocks an American accent. "Now you boys have fun," he says.

We nod. We wave. "We will," we say in unison.

Dirk continues. "Of course sex always *is* an expression of love, whether the involved parties realise it or not."

"You obviously haven't had some of the sex that I've had," I say, trying to sound knowledgeable.

"That is certainly true, but it still has some truth in it. You see the thing is..."

We spend the evening together. We eat bar-food in order to carry on talking. I am bowled over by him – bowled over by his voice, his calm; strangely bowled over by the effect it all has on me. And more than anything, I am bowled over by his beliefs about love, and sex, and life – by how important he thinks it all is. Every comment I've heard before on the subject belittles it with cynicism and irony. Dirk is different.

Thus begins our relationship. We spend three or four evenings a week together. We talk until the early hours, sometimes in a pub, sometimes in his student accommodation – complete with stuffy don furniture and various religious icons – sometimes amidst the mess of my shared house.

I discover that his father is a homophobic Methodist minister in Los Angeles. I learn that this doesn't make life easy for his gay son.

The day his birthday present arrives by post – a polyester club tie – I see him weep. "How could my folks know me so little," he says winding it around his fingers.

A little later, I manage to make him cry with laughter instead.

Sometimes we cook together, sometimes we walk together, sometimes we smoke together, but never a kiss – never even the suggestion of a kiss; never even a circumstance where a kiss could be possible. And it drives me insane. For I love him, am comfortable around him, trust him; I find our time together endlessly enthralling.

Over burnt pasta-bake – since meeting him I have apparently developed some love-induced form of Alzheimer's disease – the battle committee discusses strategy. Jenny thinks I should just pounce.

"It's obvious he's gagging for it," she says. "Christ I haven't seen you for *weeks*, you're virtually living together!"

Claire thinks I should get him drunk. "If he's just got some sort of religious hang-up then the best antidote is alcohol," she says.

I sigh; I just don't know.

We are interrupted by the telephone, it's Dirk.

I close the kitchen door on the giggling girls.

Back in the kitchen I tell my team of advisors. "He wants me to go to Brighton for the weekend."

They goggle-eye me.

"A dirty weekend in Brighton! The little devil!" says Claire.

"You said yes I take it?" asks Jenny.

I shrug. "Nah, I told him I can't go; told him I've agreed to take you to Sainsbury's."

Jenny's mouth drops. "You shouldn't have. I mean, who cares about Sainsbury's?"

I grin and shake my head. "Durhhh... As if!"

"So you accepted?"

"I did."

The girls cheer. Claire whacks me on the back.

***

The drive to Brighton takes forever. Dirk becomes hysterical every time I go over fifty miles an hour.

"I just don't feel safe in these tiny European cars," he says.

I try to point out that a Vauxhall Astra is not exactly tiny, but he doesn't seem convinced.

He has a definite penchant for history – he's mapped three castles between Cambridge and Brighton. The first one I visit with him; it reminds me of school trips. The monotone voice of the guide bores me; my feet ache within the first few seconds. The second two I sit out in the sun and smoke; it's a beautiful day.

As we leave Hastings and head for Brighton, Dirk declares that it was, "Awesome."

"I can't even begin to imagine how old that must be!" he says.

I say, "Ooh, I'd guess that it was built somewhere around ten-sixty-seven."

Dirk laughs. "Yeah, like really!" he says. His voice implies that he thinks this is a joke and I don't correct him. I marvel at the fact that even this I find cute.

The bed and breakfast is perfect: flowery bedspreads, flock wallpaper, swirly carpets and a woman in a pinny who looks like a wartime aunt from *Wish You Were Here*.

Once in the room, we drop our bags and I move towards him. I am not thinking, I am not calculating, I am quite simply *expecting* a kiss.

Dirk jokingly punches me in the stomach. He asks, "Which bed do you want?"

I smile. "Oh I don't know..." I mock.

"You want the double then," he says.

I point to it. "I was thinking that I could have this one."

I point again to the same bed. "And you could have this one."

Dirk laughs. "You're so funny!" he exclaims, disappearing into the bathroom.

I rub my forehead. I am confused. *"Great way of saying no though,"* I think.

We eat vegetarian whole-food in *Food for Friends* – I love it, Dirk hates it.

We argue about vegetarianism, politics, and religion. We disagree about everything as usual, but with Dirk I actually see this as a plus, something about the good humour, the intelligence of the discussion, the ease with which we always, eventually, agree to disagree.

We move on to a bar; I drink pints of bitter, Dirk drinks Bud. I tell him he's drinking bottled cat's piss, but he doesn't seem to care.

We go to a nightclub. A busy crowd makes the dance floor vibrate. Dirk dances frantically; his dancing has nothing to do with me – half the time he has his eyes closed, the other half he's facing the other way.

I retire to the bar and he either doesn't notice or doesn't care. I drink more beer, and when I am full of beer – when the sheer volume becomes unbearable – I switch to vodka.

Drunkenly, I talk to a lesbian from Sydney. She tells me that it's the most beautiful city in the world. She says that the gay community there is "mind-blowing." I figure I should go and visit some day.

My eyesight blurs as Dirk, laughing, appears before me. "So the deal is, I'll do the dancing, you do the drinking!" he says.

I shrug. He peers into my eyes. "Is something the matter?"

I nod at him. "I want a kiss," I whine.

He laughs.

"Don't laugh," I say, "I want a kiss... I'm sick of waiting for a kiss."

He steps back; the smile drops.

I'm having trouble pronouncing my words. I can hear myself slurring. "I love you," I say.

Dirk's eyes widen. "Well, uh..."

"What are we *doing* here anyway?" I ask.

Dirk shrugs. "Having fun?"

And finally it starts to dawn on me. "You don't even *want* to sleep with me do you? You don't even *fancy* me, do you?" I have said this too loudly; people are looking at us.

Dirk grits his teeth, then says, "You've had too much to drink."

I shake my head in despair. "Of course I've had too much to fucking drink! Otherwise I'd be sitting here in silent adoration, like the big wanker that I actually *am* instead of asking the bloody question," I say.

People are *really* staring now. Dirk glances around uncomfortably. "Can we discuss this outside please?"

He places a hand on my shoulder. I get up.

The pebbles on the beach are cold and damp. I shiver and light a cigarette. Opposite, the moon and the lights on the pier shimmer in the water. Under different circumstances it would be perfectly romantic. Still, it calms me; the cold air sobers me. "Look Dirk," I say reasonably. "I just need to know where this thing is going."

He nods his head, looks at his feet. "I'm sorry, I didn't know," he says.

"Well now you do."

"But I don't... I couldn't."

"I mean, what do you think we've been doing for two months?"

"I thought we were friends," he says.

"And you've never considered sleeping with me?"

"Sorry." He pauses. "No."

"Why?"

He shrugs. "I think I love you too much, I mean I don't really do that."

Tears well up and trickle down. "Do what?" I say. The "wh" of "what" whistles.

"I don't have relationships with people I love. I have, you know, casual sex, but not... I love you too much."

I taste the tears on my lips. "And sex as an expression of love?"

He puts a hand on my shoulder but I shrug it off.

He says, "Look, don't make this into a drama."

He says, "Let's go back to the hotel."

I say, "No." Then it turns into a shout. "Fuck off Dirk! You're just so full of shit, just fuck off."

And slowly he does; in little hesitant steps he retreats up the beach.

I weep. I sit on Brighton beach and I let it all out.

The alcohol has opened the floodgates to hell. I cry for myself, for my dead father, for anyone who has ever been unhappy. It all washes through me.

When I awaken, damp and stiff at sunrise, I return to the hotel room.

Dirk is snoring; I climb carefully into the bed but he wakes up. He moves across the bed.

A little later, he gets up and goes to the bathroom.

I pretend to sleep, but I hear him pack and then I hear him leave.

Bus Dream

The bus turns out to be wonderful. It's hard to believe that I have been driving to work for over two years. In the mornings, as it thunders down the bus-lane past the traffic-jams, I doze. In the evenings, I read. Over an hour a day gained.

I notice him on the third day; I see him climb onto the bus. He asks the driver about season tickets. He has a gentle Irish accent; his jet-black hair glistens from standing in the rain and his cheeks are ruddy. In my mind, he becomes Paddy, then Patrick. He laughs at something the driver says, moves to the back of the bus smiling at everyone, smiling at me.

I don't actually think much about it until the next morning. Not until I find myself sitting at the back of the bus, watching to see if he will climb those stairs.

He arrives at the last minute, squeezes through the closing doors. He sits in the same seat as yesterday, across from me. I sit sideways, peer at him over my book. I try to work out what's so cute about him and decide that it's his mouth – it crinkles up at the corners in a permanent smile.

He peers out of the window. Occasionally he works, scribbles what look like mathematical formulae in his notebook.

On Monday, the bus is crowded and a fat woman sits in his seat. I reserve the seat next to mine with my coat then remove it as he arrives. Our thighs bump together as the bus hammers around the roundabouts. I move my book to cover my erection. He places his coat on his own lap, and I wonder.

Tuesday, I wipe the mist from the window. I strain, hoping to see him running as the bus pulls away, dream of being the one to shout to the driver, stop the bus, save him, but he doesn't appear. I think about him all day at work and I promise fate that if he appears tomorrow I'll talk to him.

Wednesday night as I go to sleep I actually pray, beg for a second chance. I say, "Look! I know this is dumb, but that guy..." I end with, "Sorry, but there's just something about him, a feeling."

It's ridiculous, I know; for there is nothing there, no story, no opening, but it takes a month before I stop looking, stop hoping.

Eric Cantona

I've had too much to drink – Nick's friends are to blame. Two more pints are already sitting on the table, waiting for me. Nick is on form, eyes shining, an easy smile. The pub is busy, buzzy, like a London pub after work. Everything is a blur and I feel soft and cocooned by the alcohol.

"You're very quiet," says Nick.

I grin at him. "Pissed," I say.

I push through the crowd to the toilets, and as I enter, I vaguely note a new face, a *nice* face – shaved head and stubble. *"He looks like a footballer,"* I think. As I piss, the name comes to me: *Eric Cantona.*

On the way out he grins at me, a tight-lipped intentional grin with raised eyebrows.

I sit back down. "D'you know that guy by the loos?" I ask Nick.

He strains in his seat, peers over. "Which one?"

"Eric Cantona," I giggle drunkenly.

Nick stretches, stands, peers again, and sits back down. "Yeah," he says. "And I'm Marilyn Monroe!"

"He's cute though," I say. "Very... male."

Nick shrugs. "Go talk to him."

I lay my head on his shoulder. He slips an arm around me. "What's the point?" I say. "They all have a shelf life of twenty-four hours anyway. He'll be off by tomorrow."

Nick squeezes me. I pull a cigarette from the packet. "If that's the way you think," he says.

I light it. "I know, I know," I say. "I'll never meet anyone."

The smoke makes my head spin. I feel dizzy, so I stub it out and stand. "I need some air," I say.

I move clumsily through the crowd, out into the fresh night air. The roads shine beneath the drizzle; I lean against the wall. The music inside makes the windows behind me buzz and rattle. A car crawls past – the driver peers at me.

The pub door opens; the music thumps out – it's Eric Cantona. He leans against the wall beside me. He says something breathy, but it's drowned out by the music. The door closes.

"Sorry?" I ask.

"You needed fresh air too," he says. His voice is crackly, croaky.

I double take him.

He explains, touching his chest, "I lost my voice."

I nod. I stare at the streetlight opposite – it is blurred, two-headed. I shake my head.

"Sorry," I slur. "I've gotta go home... Too much to drink." I feel tired, drunk, slightly sick, slightly depressed. I can't be bothered with it at all.

Eric Cantona nods. "Can I come?" he whispers.

I turn, stare at him and try to focus. He cracks up laughing. I snigger too.

We stumble along together; I think he's as drunk as I am. It's just too much effort for him, so I talk as we bump along side by side.

He breathes "um" and "huh" noises in reply.

At home I fumble with the lock, stumble into the hall. We kiss for the first time in the darkened hallway at the bottom of the stairs, but my mouth is numbed by the alcohol – I don't feel much.

We move into the lounge. My flatmate is out, for which I am grateful. We kiss, we cuddle, we half undress, move into the bedroom. His body is tight, firm, and hairless.

We kiss again but his mouth is drunken and slobbery and I don't enjoy kissing him at all.

I fall onto my bed; he collapses beside me, rests his head on my chest.

"Look, I'm, like *really* pissed," he hisses. "I'm sorry, but..." Phlegm catches in his throat, rattles as he breathes the words.

I smile to reassure him. "Me too," I say. "There's always tomorrow morning."

I am happy just to have him in my bed.

I awaken first. I hear John rummaging around behind the bedroom door. I look at Eric Cantona lying beside me – he's smaller than I remember. He has tiny hands and darker stubble this morning. Asleep he looks quite beautiful, angelic even. I slip carefully from the bed, pull on some jeans and creep from the room.

In the kitchen, John is making tea. "D'you want some?" he asks me, waving the pot. He's wearing cricket whites.

I nod. "Two cups please."

He looks at the door, raises an eyebrow. I nod, grin.

"Tell me more," says John reaching for another cup.

I shrug. "I dunno. I was *sooo* drunk."

John pours the second cup.

"He looks a bit like that footballer, Eric Cantona," I say. "But smaller, very cute, very butch."

"His name?"

I bite my lip. "Don't know that either, husky voice though, actually he's *lost* his voice," I add, remembering.

John adds milk to the first cup of tea then pauses, interrupted by a shriek – a high-pitched, sharp-edged shriek.

"Helllooooo?"

John looks at me in surprise.

"Helllooooo! Is anyone ho-w-ome?" The voice rings around the house.

"Eric Cantona, I presume," John smirks.

I bite my lip as he appears in the doorway, a sheet wrapped around him toga-style.

"Joel actually," he says. He pronounces it "Joe-elle."

He continues, "Ooh, sorry boys." He looks at me, raises an eyebrow. "I didn't realise we had *company!*"

His voice is machine-gun speed – high pitched, exaggerated camp.

"And guess what!" he says mincing to my side.

I grit my teeth. "What?"

He flattens his hand across his chest. "I got my voice back."

He leans back against the countertop, eyes John from head to toe. "Very nice, I must say. Very... *white,*" he says.

"John plays cricket," I explain.

He purses his lips, says, "Ooh, a real man."

I look at John and imperceptibly widen my eyes.

He sees, stifles a snigger, and looks at his watch. "Oh shit!" he says.

"John?" I say. I look at him pleadingly.

"Gee, I have to go." I hear the irony in his voice.

He sweeps his cricket bag off the floor.

Eric Cantona/Joe-elle bends a leg, juts out a hip. "Oh well," he says. He sounds disappointed.

"Now you boys be good," says John pushing out of the lounge.

I roll my eyes. Under my breath I say, "Bastard!"

The front door slams and as Joe-elle spins to face me, his sheet drops. "Good morning my little cuddle-monster," he says.

He grins; his teeth need a brace.

"I have such a hangover," I say.

Gone Again

I'm in the Burleigh when I see Dirk again. I am swaying at the bar, somewhat drunk but still trying to get another round in before last orders. I grin stupidly and he smiles back.

"So, Mark!" he says. "Long time no see, how long has it been? Six months?"

We force smiles and force ourselves to laugh about Brighton.

I say, "How did you get back?" and, "I was such an arsehole."

Dirk says, "Such a good weekend, despite it all!"

But my world, suddenly, is huge again. I look at his eyes, at the sparkle of intelligence and love shining out, and it all happens to me again.

Nick appears behind me. "Are you bringing that around over or not?" he asks.

I slide an arm around Dirk's shoulders. I notice, but ignore, the rigidity of his body. I say to Nick, "He's back!"

Nick grins at us both. "Well good for you!" he says.

Dirk worms his way from my grasp, disappears into the toilets.

I chat to Nick, and Darren, and anyone else nearby, suddenly drunk and hysterically happy. When my glass is empty I point to the remaining pint on the bar, ask whose it is.

It's Dirk's. He has gone.

Mum Knows Best

Eleven-thirty p.m. It's closing time, and the house is instantly full. The three hi-fis that John has wired together, which sounded so loud when we tested them this morning, are having trouble rising above the babble of the rabble. The flashing disco lights and the smoke machine, both rented, are working in hyperactive harmony. Our lounge is a nightclub.

Forty people are frantically dancing, stomping, swinging, bouncing. Some of us, mainly my friends, are singing along with the words: *You've got to have a J.O.B. if you wanna be with me...*

Claire, strangely, is dancing the twist with the French girl currently living in her house. Owen, my brother, up for the weekend, is staring at his feet, drunkenly trying to get them to coordinate. The French girl spins Claire away into the crowd. She spins out of orbit, out of control and collapses across three people sitting on the sofa. Everyone laughs, everyone grins.

I press the button on the smoke machine and with the sound of a rush of air everything disappears behind a thick fog. I see a head floating above the grey blanket of cloud, eerily wobbling from side to side like a Hindu Deity. The only person that tall is Dirk and I grin as I move towards him.

His reaction is the same as ever: dead calm. "Hi Mark! Great party!" he says.

I restrain myself and place a hand on his shoulder. I grin at him. "I'm glad you came," I shout back. "Hey, and this time don't piss off without saying goodbye!"

Dirk laughs. "That's why I'm here," he shouts. "To say goodbye."

I frown. "Uh?"

He leans into my ear. I can feel his breath swirling around the edges as he speaks. "I'm here to say goodbye," he says. "I'm flying back to L.A. on Monday."

I nod. I force a smile.

"Everybody's gotta go sometime," I say.

"I'm sorry?" he shouts, starting to dance again.

I shrug. "Nothing," I shout.

The world seems to close around me. Dirk shuts his eyes and starts moving his tall body, swaying his head from side to side in slow circles.

I watch him. I think of Brighton. I think of every time I've seen him and wonder how I can possibly be in love with him this much.

I try to look at him objectively, try to work out one last time what is so fucking brilliant about this guy. The party swirls around me.

Dirk dances in front, oblivious as my eyes moisten. The alcohol has weakened my defences; my spirits are plummeting like a lift with a broken cable. A hand grabs my arm and I turn bleary eyed; it's Claire. She pulls me through to the kitchen.

"Come on you," she says looking at me with St Bernard eyes. "You need some air!"

We wander through the streets. No moon tonight – only tiny islands of light beneath the street lamps. The noise of the party fades into the distance. Claire hugs my arm, I can feel her shivering.

"There's nothing worse is there?" I say.

"Than what?"

"Than loving the wrong person."

She hugs my arm a little tighter. "No," she says, "there isn't." Her voice is gravelly, cracked.

I frown. I think, *"What's that all about then?"* I wonder if she's in love with John.

She's holding my arm so tightly it almost hurts. "He's stupid! I'd marry you in a second," she laughs. "I'd *snap* you up."

I look at her from the corner of my eye. She is turned towards me, she's smiling at me.

"Yeah, well, you'd be disappointed in bed," I say, trying to head it off.

She shrugs. "My Mum says that that could sort itself out," she says. "She says that the only thing that's important is loving each other."

She gives my arm a squeeze.

Internally I groan as I prise her hand from my arm. I turn to look at her. She frowns at me as I take hold of her shoulder.

"I'm afraid baby, your Mum, for once, is talking out of her arse."

Claire looks as though she might cry. Her bottom lip is sticking out slightly.

"That one *never* sorts itself out!" I say.

She looks at me, wide-eyed.

"Got it?" I say.

Claire nods miserably.

"Come on," I say. "Let's get back to that party."

Think of England

It's a dreadful winter. The rain lashes against the tin roof of the kitchen and from September onwards, we're trapped indoors. Everyone is stir-crazy, bursting with energy they can't get rid of.

Laura Ashley closes, Jenny loses her job, decides to take a year out, do the great Australian world tour thing.

She asks me to go with her, but though I am tempted, I can't – our past is too complicated. She asks Claire instead; she only takes two days to decide.

On the third of October, John and I stand in the evening rain and watch Claire's mother drive them, and their backpacks, away. I think of the three years we have been hanging out together, of the drunken parties and shopping trips, of the cups of coffee, the shared smiles, the hugs. Tears slip out mixing with the rain.

John is choked too; he can hardly speak. "The end of an era," he says dramatically.

Margaret Thatcher introduces the poll tax. Thousands of us march through the town centre shouting but no one seems to be listening.

The rain continues. John and I give up smoking outside; we blow our cigarette smoke into the extractor-fan and hope that the landlady won't smell it.

It's night-time when I drive to work, night-time when I drive home. At lunchtime when I see the half-hearted daylight, it makes me blink like a mole.

I have given up on the bus, standing in the rain is just too depressing and the mysterious, beautiful Patrick, the only reason it might have been worthwhile, never reappeared.

Late October, John is elated. He has a job in Edinburgh and he has doubled his salary overnight. I don't seem to come into the calculation.

I am amazed to be so severely slapped into place – just a mate, someone to send postcards to, but what else could I be?

Amazing to suddenly realise how peripheral we can be to other people's lives. The threads holding me centred in the middle of my own life are stretching, snapping. I start to wobble.

I go to see the doctor. He gives me a prescription for antidepressants – they are the same ones my mother takes. I don't even get it made up.

In November, John starts to remove his stuff from around the house; starts to put it in boxes that slowly fill the hallway.

In December, a week before Christmas he loads up the car, hugs me and drives away.

He says, "Come and visit."

I smile. I say, "Sure."

I feel like a jilted lover and I cry again, not for the time we have spent together, but for myself, all alone in a big house in a big town in a big cold world.

The government introduces the first homophobic law for years – books containing homosexual characters can now be removed from libraries across the country.

"History has started going backwards," says Nick.

I wish he were right, John and the girls would come back.

We march through London shouting, "No clause twenty-eight, Thatcher OUT!"

No one seems to be listening.

The winter drags on.

Strange people come to visit the house, shown around by my gushing landlady. I put a gay-pride poster in the lounge, just to make sure.

In February, Nick and Darren split up. Nick is still to be found in the Burleigh Arms every night, but now the twinkle has gone from his eyes.

Now when I say, "What's the point?" he agrees.

I get postcards from John in Edinburgh, and from the girls in Kenya, then Madagascar, India and Sydney. I line them up along the mantelpiece beneath the gay pride poster.

In March, Julia moves into the house. She brings with her, Gemma – a huge but docile Alsatian.

"Is that your poster?" she asks me.

I tell her it is.

"Oh," she says.

Her dog craps on the carpet.

When it shits on the stairs, I slip in it.

When it craps on the sofa, I explode.

Julia remains very calm. She says, "I don't suppose Gemma would have done that."

My hand trembles with the desire to slap her. I say, "Oh it was probably me then."

Julia makes floral slipcovers for the sofa, to cover the stains. "That'll cheer the place up a bit," she says.

She's always in the house, always talking drivel to her stupid, shitting dog.

In April, spring arrives and briefly the sun shines through the gaps in the clouds. Suzanne Vega comes to sing at the Corn Exchange; I am in the third row and she sings just to me. It is beautiful.

But by May, spring has turned back to winter and it seems endless. Spring is forgotten, and summer seems to have become just a vague concept.

At work the board of directors sacks my boss. "All of the slacking that has been tolerated around here is over," the new guy tells me earnestly.

So I stop working eleven hours a day, start working seven and a half.

Thank God for the summer holidays! I drive down to pick Owen up at dawn thinking about all of this. Thinking, *"Escape!"*

It's not actually raining but heavy clouds are forming in the east.

At seven a.m., we are loading his stuff into my car, and by nine-thirty we are in Calais trying to get used to driving the wrong way around roundabouts. And as we drive south it all changes, just like it used to when we were kids.

Holidays abroad were the only time when our mother ever seemed to relax. Sure she still complained, said that camping was no holiday for a mother, but she stopped bitching, she actually laughed from time to time.

The clouds thin and then vanish somewhere near Lyon.

I doze as Owen thunders down the French *autoroute*. Every time we pass a sign, move from one *department* to the next, he wakes me, he cheers.

At eight p.m., numbed by absurd amounts of driving, we roll into Aix en Provence. It is hot, thirty-five degrees, or so my car thermometer tells me – my back is stuck to the seat with sweat.

We leave the car, complete with blue tarpaulined roof rack, in the leafy shadow of the plane trees. It's a "no parking" zone but this is France.

"Such a chic street, such a tatty tarp," I think.

We drink cold beer in Les Deux Garçons. We see everyone smoking; they all look relaxed, apparently unworried by lung cancer.

Owen says, "People's body language is so different when it's hot."

"More open," I agree.

The waiter brings us a little plate of olives.

I say, "Why on *Earth* do we live in England?"

Owen laughs. "Because we're English?" he says. "Bad luck eh?"

I sip at my beer. "Maybe that's not reason enough?" I say.

Owen shrugs. "Then move."

It takes me until December to organise it all – selling the car, storing my stuff – but I plough my way through it all like a man obsessed, scared that if I think too long about it, I'll change my mind.

I leave my keys with Julia as I go, and as I pull them from my key ring I realise that there will be none left and hand her the ring as well.

The lack of keys makes me feel destitute and alone.

She stands on the doorstep with Gemma. She says, "We'll miss you." She looks genuine, but she doesn't offer to drive me to the bus station.

I adjust my rucksack and say, "Thanks." It's the best I can manage.

The walk to the bus depot takes me past the end of Andrew's house, sweet memories of the first time ever. The bus out takes me past the Burleigh Arms and on past Dirk's old place.

Quick Moves

I see him on the grainy monitor. I am sitting at the bar and, with everyone else, I look up when I hear the buzzer. The barman looks too, buzzes him in. There is something cocky, self-assured about the way he walks in, the way he pushes through the crowd – some indefinable air of everything that I hate, everything I am attracted to. I can tell, from a glance, that he's cocky, calm, collected.

He thrusts a banknote towards the barman, a lazy smile across his lips. I know that he's not boyfriend material, but still I am attracted – he's *very* French. As he waits for his drink, he scans the bar. He sees me looking at him and grins.

I move to the pool table and watch some guys playing badly. The game takes forever – the balls roll around, scrupulously avoiding the pockets. I look up and he's opposite, brown eyes looking straight at me.

He's smiling, showing white teeth and dimples, smile creases around his eyes. I could never resist a smile but when I smile back he laughs and turns away.

I walk back to the bar, swig my beer quickly and push through the crowd to the door.

It's a hot July evening and a queue of traffic is edging past the bar as I set off towards the Blue Boy.

On the door La Mamma – a terrifying fifty year old with green glitter eyeliner – extracts fifty francs from me and lets me in. The music, the smoke, the people, it all whacks me in the face. No need for a smoke machine in France – in the gay bars *everyone* smokes. In the solitary act of cruising, smoking occupies a hand during those hours of watching, waiting, hoping.

Behind the bar, four thin-camp-girly barmen are serving fast, dancing around each other. The air-conditioning can't keep up with the summer temperatures. I pull another fifty francs from my pocket and wave it, order beer.

As I proffer the banknote, a smooth voice says, "Non, c'est moi."

It's him, still smiling. "Frederic," he says, then to the barman, "Deux bières s'il vous plaît."

"You don't mind?" he asks me.

I smile. *How could I?*

We find a corner. We drink our beers, run through the basic introductory chat. He lives in Paris, he's here on holiday.

My heart flutters with disappointment; whatever this is it won't last.
He loves English men, he tells me.

My mind and instinct do battle – my dick doesn't care about long or short-term relationships.

Frederic strokes my leg, and as the balls fill, the mind empties.

"Shall I get another beer?" he asks. "Or..." He pauses. "Shall we go to your place?"

I choke on my beer.

"You want to," he says.

He's right – it is exactly what I want to do. I look around the bar to check that no one has seen this – not that I really know anyone yet anyway – then I give him my address. He has a Harley, he will follow.

At home I frantically thrust dirty washing into the laundry basket, but before I can make any impact he's here, the same face staring into another black and white monitor. I buzz him up and make one last desperate attempt at tidying – I straighten the bedcovers.

He closes the door, pulls off his motorcycle jacket and his t-shirt. "It's so hot," he says.

His chest is covered in swirls of dark hair.

I pull two beers from the tiny refrigerator and we sit on the sofa. Frederic seems relaxed; he undoes his belt, opens the buttons and starts to stroke himself. We sit on the sofa, we roll together and we kiss. His mouth is deep and wet and warm. His lips seem too soft, and I wonder briefly if he has silicon implants.

We have sex – it's wild. We throw each other around the bedroom. I wonder if all French men are like this. It's more like aerobics than sex, and I feel as though none of this has anything to do with me, as though this is just a part I am playing in a cheap porn film.

We ring the changes, do everything on my basic repertoire and some more, then we both come together in a long pumping orgasm. He kisses me, then we share his last cigarette, pulled from the pocket of his discarded jeans.

"Stay the night," I say.

"I can't," he says. "I have to go back, I've got a plane to catch tomorrow morning."

My eyes widen. "Tomorrow!" I say. "I mean I knew... But you didn't say *tomorrow!*"

As I watch him dress, I try to get a handle on how I feel. The sex was so good I'm having trouble being objective.

He looks at me, strokes my chin, and kisses me. It seems a shame to end it there.

He says, "Don't worry."

We swap numbers.

He says, "I'll call you tomorrow when I get home."

From the balcony I watch him ride away. I raise my hand and he waves back.

I am happy for a while – I play some music, stare at the moon, and smile. *"I will feel no guilt,"* I tell myself. *"Take the joy wherever it is to be found,"* I say.

Quite consciously I try to push the worries, the doubt away. But slowly the moment evaporates and I am left feeling emptied and dreadful.

I wake up feeling depressed and decide to call him to leave a cutesy message on his answer phone, but I've made an error writing down his phone number.

So I wait for him to call, all day, all week.

I try the number twice a day but it's always wrong.

Then after two weeks I wonder about the motorbike. *"If he flew from Paris, then where did the Harley come from?"*

Only when friends arrive for their summer holidays a month later do I completely forget him.

I take them to Vence, half an hour from my apartment.

We choose a bar for lunch and we sit.

The Mediterranean sun beats down, prickling our skin despite the canopy.

A waiter appears in the doorway behind me. "Bonjour Monsieur-Dame," he says. "Are you having lunch or just drinks?"

The voice is rich and smooth; I know it and turn. I say, "No!" I say, "Shit."

"Ah Non!" he says. "Merde!"

Frederic grins at me as though this is funny. I shake my head at him – speechless. We move to another restaurant.

My German Heroin

The party is heaving, maybe eighty people are milling, dancing, and drinking their way around the white-walled, loft apartment.

The difficult part is over; we have stood in the empty room, stared unnerved at the row of chairs along the lounge wall, remembered awful school discos, but now we have got through it – people have filled the space.

The music has crept up decibel by decibel to fill the air, and Yves' pure-alcohol-but-tastes-like-orange-juice punch has melted the taut edges around people's mouths into laughter and smiles.

I'm standing, swaying to the music – some eighties disco stuff remixed to sound happening – and Yves, our host, my French teacher, arrives, towing him behind, laying him eagerly at my feet.

"Mark, meet Pierre, my oldest school friend." With this he winks at me and grooves into the midst of the dancers.

Pierre is good looking, in fact good looking enough that normally I would blush and clam up, but lubricated by a mixture of rum, gin, vodka, martini and orange juice I slip easily, and with pleasure, into the set-up. "Bonsoir," I say.

He's small, maybe one metre seventy, dark Mediterranean skin, with spiky gelled-to-look-wild hair, a small goatee beard, big smile, white teeth, big silver hoops in each ear. He's wearing a fluorescent green shirt and frayed jeans.

"So you're Yves' Rosbeef student," he grins. His accent is thick, slightly camp, very Niçois, filled with laughter or mockery, I'm not sure which.

I smile. "And you've known Yves for hundreds of years then," I say.

He nods. "My oldest froggy friend." He steps in closer to me. "The first person I ever met in France."

"I thought you were French," I say.

He laughs. "No, Greek." He winks at me. "And you know what they say about the Greeks." A jiving blond woman bashes into his back, throws him against me – I catch him. When we separate, a mischievous, diabolical grin spreads across his face.

"So why did you and Yves never get it together?" he asks. "If you're as wonderful as he says you are?"

Yves is passing behind me carrying drinks to some new arrivals.

"Be careful how you answer," Yves says. "Your life may just depend on it."

"Because he's an arsehole," I reply.

Pierre smiles and whisks a drink from Yves' hand as he passes. "You see," he tells him, "I told you we'd get on fine, we already have something in common. We both think you're an arsehole."

Yves laughs and boogies away with the drinks.

More people arrive, until all the rooms of his apartment are filled.

Pierre and I alternate between dancing (he dances well) and chatting (he's funny, witty, irreverent).

He tells me about his job, he works as a Minitel host.

Minitel is an exception Française, a sort of black and white, character only terminal dished out by France telecom since the sixties. It's a kind of pre-Internet with its main difference being that connection to services, similar to Internet sites, is billed per minute by France telecom at, depending on what your doing, more or less exorbitant rates.

Pierre explains that he works on a Minitel dating server, the prehistoric equivalent of the Internet chat room. He's paid to look at people's CVs, work out what they're hoping to find, and then connect to the server pretending to be Mr (or Mrs) Right.

This explains to me why whenever I've tried the services, I have never managed to get a real date. It also explains why people here have such terrifying Minitel bills at the end of the month.

Pierre tells me that earlier this week he got confused while talking to a recently divorced school-teacher on one server, and a leather-clad gay masochist slave on another. The poor schoolteacher disconnected when Jennifer – the recently bereaved thirty-year-old woman he had been pretending to be – suddenly offered to tie him to the bedposts, put pegs on his nipples and stick a cucumber up his arse.

"The slave boy on the other hand didn't seem to mind at all when I asked him if he had ever thought of remarrying," Pierre laughs.

"I never managed to get a date on any of those," I tell him.

"People rarely do. You were probably chatting to me," he laughs. "You know," he continues, leaning in towards my ear. "I would *love* to take you home and put pegs on your nipples."

I raise my hand to protect myself and grin at him in amazement. "Ouch!" I say.

He grabs my arm. "Come!" he says. "We can talk better outside."

I pull my sweatshirt down to cover my stirring interest and follow him to the door. As we push out of the apartment, Pierre snatches a joint from a German woman sitting on the stairs. She says something to us in German – something rude probably, but then German always sounds aggressive to me. We head down into the street.

I sit on a bollard. Above us, from an open window, we can hear the party thumping. Pierre hands me the joint; I take a drag.

40

He asks, "Do you live near here? Can we go to your place?"

I look up at him but his face seems distorted. It strikes me that it is an exceptionally hot evening. My face prickles and my mouth fills with a strange acidic taste. My teeth taste disgusting, my saliva seems electric.

Pierre crouches in front of me. "Are you OK? God! You're soaked!" he says.

Sweat is rolling down my face, dripping from my chin. My head flops forward. For some reason I am crying, tears dribbling from my eyes.

Pierre lifts my head so that I am looking at him. The joint drops to the floor, seemingly in slow motion, turning and spinning as it falls.

"You are so white," he says.

"I don't feel..." I say.

And then it happens; it is instant and unexpected. The vomit squirts through my teeth. Pierre leaps back from me, but he's too late. His eyes look down at his shirtfront in horror, then up at me.

He says, "Jesus."

I sleep until four in the afternoon.

When I awaken, I feel shaky and vague; I don't remember how I got home. There is a note on the table, it says, "Hope you feel better. Pierre." It's followed by a phone number.

I eat a bowl of cold pasta from the fridge, which I immediately throw up, then climb back into my bed where I sleep, non-stop, for another fifteen hours.

The next day I'm too embarrassed to call him and the day after that I actually feel too embarrassed that I didn't call him the day *before*, so I decide to try to forget the whole thing.

The following Saturday, Yves phones me, and adds me to his list of people who fell ill after smoking the joints supplied by the mysterious German woman.

"She killed the whole party," he says. "Between those who smoked her shit and were ill, and those that carried them home, I lost half of the people who were here!"

I hang up and consider calling Pierre - consider telling him this as some kind of alibi, but as I move my hand over the phone, it rings.

"Hello," he says. I can hear him smiling. "Are you better?"

"Yes, a bit," I say.

"Yves tells me that you only vomit on your dates when you've been smoking heroin," he says.

"Heroin?" I gasp.

"Uhuh!" he says. "Apparently so."

Medieval Obsessions

An hour later we are in a restaurant eating pizza together. He's as I remember him, witty and cute. "Not a very good start really," I say.

"The I-Ching calls this kind of thing, *Difficulty at the beginning leads to supreme success,*" he replies.

"Umh," I think, *"he reads the I-Ching."* I always like a bit of mysticism in a man.

Our knees touch under the table and his physical proximity arouses me. He regales me again with new tales of dialogue from his strange job, tells me he has spent most of the morning talking to a nymphomaniac dominatrix whose husband doesn't know and wouldn't understand.

In the afternoon he chatted to a husband whose wife has lost all interest in sex and who as a result is looking for a mistress to try, "the things his wife would never understand." We laugh wondering if maybe the two are married.

We drink a lot of wine with the meal, but I'm careful to stop before I get drunk, terrified of throwing up a second time.

I have a hard-on beneath the table; I can't wait to get back to the apartment and see where all of this will go, how the story will unfold. I like him, I fancy him, and something intrigues me about the strange little twinkle in his eye – something to do with his eye contact lasting just a fraction longer than normal, as if asking an unspoken question, trying to spot something within me. I offer him a cup of tea at my place.

He giggles. "You English and your tea," he laughs.

We walk the three blocks to my apartment. The streets are Monday-night empty. As we walk, the sexual tension between us strikes me as unbearable.

I consider kissing him in a doorway, but I wait.

We chase up the stairs to the apartment and burst, laughing for no reason, into my kitchen. Pierre closes the door with his arse, and stands passively leaning against it, waiting.

I throw the keys on the countertop and kiss him.

He doesn't want my tongue in his mouth, nor his in mine, so we are reduced to a strange non-sexual pecking.

He pulls my t-shirt off; I unbutton his beige shirt. I spot a pierced nipple and pull back the shirt to examine it more closely.

He laughs. "Did you never see one before?"

I shrug. "No, not in the flesh."

"So?" he asks.

I touch it tenderly. "Does it hurt? I mean, is it sensitive?"

He pulls on the ring. "Not at all, you see..."

I pull on it. "So that doesn't hurt."

Pierre stares into my eyes. "Not at all," he says quietly, his pupils dilating. "It's what they're for."

I grin. "They?"

I undo the remaining shirt buttons revealing two more identical rings on his other nipple and his belly button.

"Wow," I say.

Five rings, one in each ear, one in each nipple and one through his belly button. I stand back and look at him leaning against the door.

"So you like them?" he asks.

I nod. "Yeah, very sexy," I say.

I'm actually not sure; he looks a bit like a Christmas tree. I move back in and pull on both nipples simultaneously.

Pierre half closes his eyes – he looks drugged, he groans. I unbutton his jeans, and with a strange sense of foreboding slide them down. His dick is large, half hard, weighed down by a huge chrome ring through the head, at least three centimetres in diameter.

"Awww, Jesus!" I say, "Now that one *must* hurt."

Pierre smiles placidly, slips a finger through the ring and yanks his dick from side to side. "Not at all," he says.

I crouch down to examine it more closely. "But you can't put a condom on."

He shrugs. "I don't need to, I don't fuck."

"Can you suck it?"

"Is this a biology class?"

I stand up again. "Sorry, I just don't know, I mean I never..."

Pierre pushes me back down. "No, I can't suck it," he says. "But you can."

I try. The heavy ring bangs against my rear teeth; it feels as though they might chip. The contact with my fillings gives me little electric shocks – like aluminium paper on chocolate, it's horrible. I give up and stand, try to push him to his knees, but he resists.

"I don't suck," he says.

I pull him through to the bedroom; push him onto the bed. He folds his arms behind his head, watches me remove my trainers, shuck my jeans.

I lie on top of him, rub my body against his hairy chest, feel his piercings against my body. He remains immobile.

I slide a hand between his legs. He doesn't move to help or hinder access.

I slide a finger against his anus; he removes a hand from behind his head to stop me.

"I'm not into anal," he says.

I close my eyes and try not to get annoyed, but it's too late, the moment has passed. I give up and roll off him.

"What's wrong?" he asks.

"Thirsty," I say.

I stand, go through to the kitchen and fill a glass with water from the tap.

When I come back he's standing up. He still looks great.

"So?" he asks.

"So..." I take a deep breath. I sip my water. "Look, I erm... well I don't really get what you *do* do in bed, I mean, you don't suck, you virtually can't be sucked with that thing through your dick, you can't fuck, you don't like to be fucked, you barely kiss. Sorry, but what *do* you do?"

Pierre moves towards me. He takes my hand, kisses it, and slides it to his cheek. He stares into my eyes; his dick hardens. His pupils seem huge, black and bottomless.

"Slap me," he says.

I frown.

"Slap my face."

I pull my hand away from his cheek in horror. "No!"

"Just gently if you want, but slap my face."

I shrug again. "But I don't want to."

He grabs my two hands. "Please, slap me," he implores me. "I like it."

For a moment I think, *"What the hell! Why not?"* I actually try to move my arm to do it, but strangely, in the end I am physically incapable. Something within me won't let me do it – my arm blocks.

"I can't." I move away. "I need to piss," I say.

He holds on tightly to my arms. "No, stay," he says.

"But I need to piss."

He grins. "Exactly..." He kneels before me.

I close my eyes to try to think. I laugh.

I say, "OK! Look! This is ridiculous."

He looks at me questioningly.

"This isn't going to work at all," I say. I push his hands away; walk through to the bathroom.

When I return he has dressed. "I think I better go," he says.

He walks to the front door, pecks me on the cheek. "Shame," he says grinning.

He looks like the man I brought here half an hour ago. The well dressed funny, good-looking, normal man. "Yes," I agree. "A real shame."

He opens the door, steps out, and then turns back. "If you ever..." he pauses.

I smile. "Yes?"

"Well... if you ever, you know, mellow out – I mean about your sexuality."

I take a breath. "I wasn't aware I had a problem with my sexuality," I say.

"Well, no," he laughs. "Apart from the fact that that you have like this medieval oral-anal obsession."

I lift a hand and wave at him.

I say, "Au revoir." I say it gently, and with extreme concentration I manage to quietly close the door in his face.

It takes a few minutes for me to get really angry, to wish that I *had* slapped him. Medieval oral-anal obsession indeed!

Roberto di Milano

I am standing at the bar, waiting to be served. I hate the Blue Boy, hate the dingy corners, the tiny dance floor, and the steps that I am forever tripping up and down, but Le Klub is closed for their annual holiday, so I have no choice.

I wave my banknote; try to squeeze in a little closer to the bar. The guy to my right blows cigarette smoke up into the air, but the air conditioning pushes it down into my eyes.

It looks like a bar from another era, from a time when bars were illegal, and so, by definition, underground and grotty. I look to my right – a Dame Edna Everage look-alike is sitting at the bar with a poodle. I scan to the left – a few guys are lined up against the wall, leaning, waiting, watching.

The hairs on the back of my neck prickle, I run a hand across them.

The barman tugs at the banknote in my hand to get my attention.

I order a gin and tonic and look behind me and see why I have been feeling uncomfortable – he's leaning against the wall behind me. He's staring at me, at me alone. I glance back to the barman, hand over my banknote; pick up my drink.

As I turn, he grins at me, raises his eyebrows and raises his glass. He seems huge, a great larger than life, brick-chicken-shed of a man.

I feel very tarty, very direct, but, as Nick used to say, *"I just can't help myself."*

Once I cross the bar he's not as big as he seemed – my height, but oh, what a body! I nod, slightly embarrassed. "Bonsoir," I say.

He's Italian. He introduces himself as, "Roberto. Roberto *di Milano.*"

I don't know if he's from Milan, or if that's his surname, or maybe both. I resist the temptation to introduce myself as, *Marco. Marco di Eastbourne.*

He speaks a little French, but with an accent and oh what an accent! A thick, rich, deep, luxurious, velvet-pile-carpet of an accent. It's on the edge, almost too much, slightly too greasy, like a three cheese pizza – delicious but just a bit indigestible.

I ask him what sport he does; use the occasion to touch a finger against his chest. It has been calling to me, whispering to me through the semi-transparent linen.

"Negation," he says, apparently mixing his words. After a brief mime I understand that he's a swimmer. That he's a member of the

Milan gay swimming team. His three-quarter length trousers reveal calves to match his torso. He grins revealing perfect white teeth.

"J'aime les inglésé," he says.

It seems obvious that we will sleep together, it's buzzing around in the air between us. His perfection annoys me slightly, or is it the fact that he knows it, the fact of his arrogance?

"Where do you live?" I ask. "I bet you live with your mother." I am intentionally teasing him, trying to see what happens if we sidestep the smooth talk.

He frowns at me. "Why should I live with my mother?" he asks.

I shrug. "Every Italian man I ever met lives with his mother," I say, matching his grin.

Roberto shakes his head. "It's just a stereotype. It's not true."

I nod. "So where do you live?"

"In Milan. With my mother." Apparently he sees no irony in this reply. He smiles at me, runs the back of his hand down the front of my shirt.

"And you?" he asks.

"In Nice," I reply. "Alone."

Roberto winks at me. "Maybe you show me?" he says.

I go to the toilet. I calculate the pros and cons: a bit of a slime ball, very good-looking, very good body, very keen. In the end the calculation doesn't take long – I can't resist.

"So you show me?" he repeats when I return.

I laugh at the directness of it all.

Roberto frowns. "You don't want maybe?"

It is the final disarming straw. He *is* human. I smile to reassure him. "Don't worry," I say. "I want!"

Roberto is *hot*. Roberto is in a hurry.

With his hand constantly hovering around my crotch it's hard to drive. With his face constantly stuffing itself in front of mine it is difficult to see the road. I push him away; I try to do it jokingly.

"We'll be home in *minutes*," I tell him.

He slides a hand over my thigh. I pick it up, move it back onto his own lap. "Mamma Mia!" I say. "Will you please wait?"

Roberto giggles. He grabs my hand, places it on his own crotch – I discover that he's terrifyingly well endowed.

"There has to be a problem," I say to myself, glancing across at him. There's always a problem, it just takes a moment before you find it.

"I want you to suck me," Roberto says in a perfect American accent.

Amazing how many people around the world speak perfect porno-film English. I laugh and put the car into reverse. "We're home," I say. "WAIT!"

I turn off the engine. Roberto leans over, places a hand behind my head and thrusts his tongue down my throat; his hand fumbles with my zip. I pull away again; push out through the door of the car. I sigh at him, shake my head.

Roberto jumps out too. His eyes glint madly at me and I realise that he's wearing coloured contact lenses. His eyes have taken on a zombie shine in the orange light of the street. I walk towards the house.

"I want you to suck me!" he repeats.

I laugh to myself. "It's just not possible," I say under my breath.

He repeats himself, louder, "I want you to suck me!"

I bite my lip. I grin at him. "Quiet!" I look around at my neighbours' windows. *"Please?"*

The street is silent and empty. A single man is walking towards us, head down. I fumble with the key in the glass door and then push it open. I turn to Roberto to let him enter. His trousers have dropped to half way down his thighs. His dick is jutting out at me, huge and proud.

"Jesus!" I exclaim. I glance nervously at the guy coming along the street, grab Roberto's arm and pull him into the lobby.

The glass door closes slowly behind him.

"What is wrong with you?" I shake my head.

"I like," says Roberto, grinning, leaning back against the glass door.

"Please, pull your..." I reach down to pull his trousers back up.

He grabs my head, pulls it towards him.

"Yeah, suck that big fat dick," he says.

I catch a glimpse of the man in the street peering in at us, then hurrying by. I imagine what he sees – Roberto's butt against the glass, me bending down before him. *"Must look well dodgy,"* I think. *"It is well dodgy,"* I think.

I stand; fight to pull his trousers up. He laughs hysterically.

A door opens upstairs, a woman's voice says, "OK then. See you later." – *"A toute à l'heure."*

"Shit, my neighbour! Will you just?"

Roberto grins madly at me, his eyes flash. "I like!" he repeats.

I pull away; start to walk up the stairs. I hope he will dress and follow me. On the landing I meet my neighbour, the schoolteacher.

We say, "Bonsoir." We smile politely.

I try to sound as low key as possible. If Roberto is still nude maybe she'll think he's nothing to do with me. I open my apartment door listening for news from below. I hear nothing.

The front door opens, closes. I wait in the doorway – nothing.

I quietly climb back down the stairs, peer around the corner into the entrance-hall – no one.

I open the front door; look right then left. I am just in time to see Roberto di Milano round the corner with my neighbour; I can hear that they are talking. I lie awake till five a.m. wondering what about.

48

City of Angels

I sit in front of the boss. I fiddle with a cufflink – they are shaped like taps; they turn. I watch him humbly wring his hands in pseudo anguish. It's a ridiculous game; he knows I have been travelling too much, that I am exhausted. I know that he's building up to send me somewhere else, probably too soon, too far and that I will refuse.

He already knows what he will offer me to make me accept, but in the meantime we have to play The Game.

"And so you see," he says re-wringing his hands, "some of these newer clients could turn out to be very important for us."

I stare out of the window at the clear blue sky. I watch the leaves fluttering in the midday sunlight. It's so hard to work down here when you're used to one sunny day a month, so hard to remember that everyday is a sunny day. I wonder why we have to work, why we can't spend our days wandering through the forest gathering nuts.

"Progress!" I think.

He's trying to make me feel important now. Anyone listening would imagine I am James Bond instead of a bank-note distributor salesman.

"And so you see," he continues, "you're the only person I can count on."

I glance at my watch, smooth my shirt-cuff back over it. "Look. Mr Soda," I interrupt.

He folds his hands on the desk, leans forward earnestly. "Tell me what's on your mind Mark," he says.

It reminds me of a computer program we used to have at college, Eliza. It gave the resemblance of a conversation by saying, "Tell me about it," and "How do you feel about it?" and other such inanities. I wonder briefly if my boss is an android. The thought makes me smirk; I stifle it.

"Could we just get to the where and the when? You know I only got back from Hong Kong yesterday. I'm extremely tired. I haven't even *unpacked* yet!"

He nods. "Of course, Mark, sorry. Los Angeles," he says. "Now they're very..."

I stop listening and think of Dirk. Even now, years later, say, *America,* or *tall,* or *California,* or *love of my life,* and I think of Dirk.

I wonder how I can get his address, wonder if he's still in L.A. I say, "Sure, when?"

49

Mr Soda frowns at me. "Oh, erm, Wednesday."

I groan. "Wednesday! What, *this* Wednesday?"

He clenches his teeth, nods as if to say, *I'm really sorry about this.*

I shrug. "OK."

He looks at me like a kid who just found out he's getting a bicycle for Christmas.

"But I need two things," I say.

He nods again.

"I need today and tomorrow to rest, I need sleep, so you'll have to get someone else to finish the Hong Kong stuff."

He nods. "That's fair."

"And I need Carol to track down an old friend of mine in Los Angeles. I don't have his number any more."

He nods. "Give me the name," he says, "I'll make sure she does it."

I pull his Post-It pad towards me. I write, *Dirk Flaubert.* "Shouldn't be too hard," I say. "I don't suppose that there are a lot of Flauberts in Los Angeles. I'm sure Moneypenny can handle it."

He frowns at me. "Sorry?"

I shrug. "Nothing." I straighten my tie. I stand. "I'll call in tomorrow to pick up the sales packs," I say.

He nods. "Thanks Mark!" he says. "You're our star player you know!"

I turn towards the door. I roll my eyes and internally I groan.

***

It's a risky strategy, and when my second visit fails I start to wonder if he has a boyfriend who he stays with, if he has gone away on vacation, if he has moved away, died...

I wonder if I will ever catch him in. I know I could have organised this differently, I know I could have called, but in some way I have chosen to leave it to fate.

I stand; I reach out, press the buzzer. It's my third visit to his apartment. *"If this is meant to happen,"* I think, *"then he'll be in."* And if he's in then it's *a sign.* It's the kind of logic my grandmother used to use.

The intercom crackles, then nothing, a false alert. I sigh; I turn away.

"Yes?" asks a metallic voice behind me.

Beneath my breath I say, "Yes!" I turn back to the intercom. "Dirk Flaubert?"

"Sure. And you are?"

I can tell, even through the intercom, that his voice hasn't changed – that he still has that relaxed Californian drool. I grit my teeth, put on my best American accent. "FedEx," I say. "Delivery for Mr Flaubert."

50

I hear him say, "Oh!" He sounds surprised. He sounds excited.

"I'll be right there," he says.

I stand to one side of the glass doors, peer to the back of the lobby, wait for the door to move. *"Surprise, surprise!"* I think.

A light comes on; I wait. A door opens and I see him walking towards me. As he reaches for the door handle he pauses, looks at me through the glass, frowns.

"Hey!" he says aggressively. "Didn't you say FedEx?"

I nod. "Sure did."

He smiles at me, frowns at the same time. He opens the palms of his hands towards me as if to say, *So? What's the score?*

He has put on a lot of weight since I last saw him; he's grown a beard and gained a pair of glasses as well. He looks very ordinary; very middle America. I sigh; let the accent drop.

"Dirk?" I whine. "Don't you recognise me at all?"

A smile of recognition ripples across his face. His mouth opens into a smile of amazement. "Mark?" He opens the door, looks at me with lunatic eyes. "What the hell?"

I shrug. "I was in your neighbourhood."

He opens the door wide, pulls me in. "That is so cool!" he says. "I mean, how did you find me, and how come you're in L.A., and what's with the suit? Jees! Come up, come up... God I'm sorry!"

The apartment is far better than the anonymous grey-faced building suggests. Maybe a thousand square feet, divided up with half height walls into living, dining, kitchen, and sleeping areas. The walls are white or deep Bordeaux red. A comfortable jumble of books and magazines covers every surface.

"Sorry about the, erh," he says, removing Psychology Today from the sofa.

I smile. "I'm not likely to complain. You remember my place!"

He grins at me, visibly relaxing. "I do!" he says.

I hang my jacket over the chair back. He slumps on the sofa. He's wearing baggy half-length shorts and an oversize sweatshirt. His added weight seems to make him even taller, his legs even huger. "So! You're here with your job then?"

I look him over with a critical eye, think, *"He's not so cute."* I loosen my tie and roll my sleeves. I tell him about my job, about the clients, life in France, a couple of amusing boyfriend stories. He tells me he hasn't been seeing anyone, not for years.

"I feel like I've been crossing the desert," he says. "Still, I have to get to the other side at some point, right?"

I smile. "Or at least to an oasis," I say.

We talk for nearly two hours. We drink so much coffee my hands start to shake. We arrange to spend Saturday together.

"My turn to show *you* around," says Dirk.

His car is a huge lolloping rust-coloured saloon. We shuffle along in a series of traffic jams towards Sunset Boulevard. In my head I see the cover of a Don Henley album: palm trees and sunsets and magic.

The reality – a grimy street with no architectural cohesion and a beggar at every set of lights reminds me more of a European industrial zone than a city of angels.

"The problem with L.A.," explains Dirk, "is that there's nothing to actually *see*, well, except for smog and bag-ladies. The rest is just myth. America's finest, but myth all the same."

He points out the church where Bing Crosby got married, Judy Garland's school, the Charlie Chaplin studios. I nod, try to sound excited, but the overriding experience is of sitting in a traffic jam. Dirk takes me up past immaculate lawns to see the Hollywood sign. It too, is better when set to music beneath a pink sunset; today it just looks like a shabby set of letters plonked on a hill.

"When they legalised Marijuana some jokers changed it to Hollyweed," Dirk tells me.

We lean on the railings side by side. We look at the buildings rising above the smog.

"You get great sunsets here though," he says, "what with the pollution and all."

A tiny breeze blows his blond mop into his eyes. Our arms touch slightly.

I say, "Don't you ever regret Europe, or anywhere else for that matter? Places with clean air, calm..."

Dirk stares out over the city. "I regret loads of stuff," he says. "But mainly people, not so much places."

His deep voice still makes my chest vibrate. His easy open manner still strikes me as infinitely loveable.

"I know what you mean," I say. But the moment that I say it, it has happened again. It is suddenly as if we have been apart for twenty-four hours instead of four years and I am in love with him as I was every other time I ever saw him. My heart swells and feels as though it could burst with the joy of being with him, being here, being alive. The view of Los Angeles is suddenly majestic and beautiful and my eyes are watering.

Dirk looks at me, concern in his eyes. "Hey Mark, I didn't mean... I mean, I wouldn't want you to think..." he says.

And so with the love comes the pain. The pain of wondering if he has ever loved me. Wondering if it's possible that someone I have always known so clearly that I love, can really feel nothing for me at all. Wondering if there will ever be anyone else in the entire world that I will feel so easily, happily comfortable around.

I'm here for this and this alone. *"The moment must not pass,"* I think. "Dirk, can I ask you something?" I say.

He nods, he laughs. "Sure."

"Something personal, something difficult?"

"Sure," he repeats.

"Thanks, it's important to me, no matter the answer."

"So?" He raises an eyebrow at me.

"Well, just out of interest, say, *historical* interest... Did you *ever* love me?" I ask him. I am pleased with my voice. It sounds almost relaxed, disinterested, easy-come, easy-go.

Dirk blows through his lips. He nods, staring into the distance. "I guess I did," he says. "In a way."

I frown; I stare straight ahead. "What way?" I ask.

He shrugs again.

"Try," I say. "It's important for me to know."

He sucks air through his teeth. It sounds as though he's thinking about a technical problem.

"I suppose in a kind of sacred way, a religious way," he says.

I frown and stop breathing. I wait.

"As a fellow human being," he says. "As someone I... liked, someone I... cared about."

He nods to himself, lost in memories and apparently happy with his explanation. I breathe out, nod very slightly. My eyes are tearing and my nose is starting to run.

"And as a friend," he says. "I would have liked us to be closer, to spend more time together..."

I nod. I swallow. "Me too," I say. My stomach feels knotted.

"So why..." I search for words. "Why weren't we? Closer I mean?"

Dirk swallows and glances behind him. He changes his posture against the railings; his shoulder no longer touches mine. "You were in love with me!" he says. "It was different for you. I tried to be clear, maybe I wasn't. It's not always easy."

I closed my eyes. "Clear about what?" I say.

"Well, that I've never, you know, seen you in that way."

I nod.

Dirk continues, "I never had, you know, the desire to... well, to sleep with you I suppose."

I nod again.

"I mean I could just *never...*"

I interrupt him. "OK, OK! I think I got it," I say. My voice sounds croaky and dry.

Dirk laughs. "Sorry," he says.

"And did you sleep with anyone else... during your year? I mean, I know that's not my business, it's just to try to understand."

Dirk shrugs again, he nods. "Sure, no problem, well, yeah, I did, a few..."

"A few?" I repeat.

"Sure, maybe ten, twenty guys, during the whole year."

I nod. I receive this news like a slap around the face with a wet towel. I had never even imagined this. It had never even crossed my mind. I wonder who they were, wonder where he met them, wonder what they had that was so much better than me, or seeing as there's maybe twenty of them, what I have that is so *terrible*... It sounds like I am the only person he met in Cambridge that he *couldn't* bring himself to sleep with. The information reels and rolls around in my head.

He drapes a huge arm across my shoulder. "I wouldn't wanna be accused of not being clear again!" he says.

I look around, searching for a reason to escape. On my left I see two Japanese tourists. One of them is holding a camera, patently hoping that someone will offer to take the photo; I wriggle from beneath Dirk's arm. "You want your photo taken?"

The girl smiles at me broadly, nods twice. She wraps her arm around her girlfriend.

I position the word HOLLYWOOD above their heads. My eyes are watery, my vision blurred. I can see Dirk through the viewfinder to the left of the girls – he's grinning at me. *"He has no idea!"* I think.

I press the shutter release. The girls grin and bow in thanks, then one of them points at my camera. "And you... You friend?" she asks.

Her friend nods enthusiastically. "Yes, now you!" she agrees.

I shake my head. "Nah, It's OK."

"Yes," she insists. Her friend nods again.

I sigh and hand her the camera. I move next to Dirk; he puts an arm around my shoulder again. "Are you OK?" he asks, hugging me tightly to his side.

I grin at the camera, a big cheesy grin. "Great," I say.

"Never again," I think. *"I must never put myself through this again."*

Italian Duo

As I walk towards La Civette, I scan the tables, looking for empty space. The town is balmy and filled with Italian tourists – it must be a bank holiday over the border.

There are two free tables; one is next to a woman in her fifties – straight, black-bob haircut, elegantly dressed, reading a book. She looks at me as I approach. The second table is next to... I double take. I almost run to make sure I get the table. He's beautiful, he's huge – he's the proverbial Adonis. I choose the chair that half faces him.

He glances at me, then returns to a texting operation on his mobile phone. I watch him text, I watch him smoke. I look at his huge hands, the light blond hair on his arms, the shine on his shaved head, the dimples on either side of his mouth. I watch him watch me watching him.

I think of a song, Dr Feelgood: *I was looking back to see if she was looking back to see if I was looking back at her.* It rolls around in my head.

I roll a cigarette and order beer; the sun beats down. The woman with the book keeps glancing over at me so I try to avoid her gaze. I search for my lighter, search *desperately* for my lighter.

I don't have a lighter; it never fails. He leans over, offers me his matches. His eyes are grey, piercing in the middle of his olive, tanned face. His teeth glint a smile at me, he strokes his chin. I smile; I thank him.

He moves his chair slightly as he sits back. A calculated, natural accident, which points him a full thirty degrees further towards me.

My beer arrives; he raises his in a vague toasting gesture. We smile.

We watch the hordes; we see a juggler, followed by a street acrobat. A jazz band appears and busks in front of us. Their smiling and joking around makes me feel like I'm on holiday. The sax player is cute. I look at him for a moment, he grins at me.

But he's nothing on the Italian. We both watch the band and we watch each other watching.

I'm supposed to go to the shops before they shut but I can't leave, not before the end of the film, not before I see what, if anything, is going to happen. I order food here instead; the man does too. He laughs as he orders, making the waiter laugh too.

Our orders arrive together. We've both chosen "Norwegian" salads: salmon, prawns, lettuce... We grin; we raise eyebrows.

The waiter brings beer but I still have one, so I tell him I didn't order it. He points to the Italian who is grinning at me. "He sent it," the waiter tells me.

We eat at our separate tables. It seems rude after such a gallant gesture but I can't find the courage to invite him to move.

He goes to the toilet and I see the real enormity of him – my height but a body builder, ninety kilos at least, and no fat, absurdly huge. His arms must be the width of my legs. He has the best bubble-butt I have ever seen. The flaps on his rear pockets jut out horizontally.

I finish my salad and as he returns he leans on the chair opposite me. "Je peux?" he asks. His accent in French is thick, pure Italian.

The gesture is so up-front yet so polite, I laugh. "Sure." I nod.

As he sits I see a bulge in the front of his military trousers.

"Thanks for the drink," I say.

I feel a stirring between my own legs. I cross them.

He smiles at me, holds out a hand. "Fabrizio," he says.

"Mark."

He's so big he blocks any view I might have of anything. It's not so bad, except that I feel so tiny; I sit up straighter.

I try to think of something to say. "Are you here on holiday?" It's banal but I say it anyway.

He shrugs, he grins.

I try in French, *"Vous êtes ici en vacances?"* He shrugs again.

I order a beer for my new friend. He says something long, something complicated to me in Italian.

I shrug; I smile. "Sorry?" I say.

He sips his beer and thinks for a while.

"You like me," he says hesitantly.

I grin; I nod. "I don't really know you, but, sure, you seem very nice," I say.

He smiles, he shrugs. I ask if he prefers English or French. "Italiano," he says.

I smile; I shrug.

"So, you like me," he says again earnestly.

"Jees, how do you say cute in Italian?" I wonder. "Molto, cuto... erh, mignono?" I say.

He shrugs; frowns, and I give up on any hope of subtlety. "Yes," I say.

He asks something else in Italian. He winks at me, it is an earnest question and he seems embarrassed to ask it. I hear something like *amora.* I guess it means love. I compute the possibilities; *I love it here don't you? I want to make love to you?*

The sax player holds a hat in front of me and I put ten francs in it. He winks at me, shoots me a cheeky grin, and moves on. I subconsciously notice that he really *is* cute.

"Sex," says Fabrizio leaning in. He nods and arches his eyebrows, points at himself, then at me, then away to his left.

I feel myself blush. Without being able to make a joke of it I don't know how to respond so I shrug. Fabrizio looks sad.

I think, *"I may never, ever, have another chance to sleep with someone who looks like this."* I nod. "Si," I say.

Fabrizio grins, then stops, rolls his eyes and opens his hands to the sky. He actually says, "Mamma Mia!"

A woman is pushing through the tables towards us – long, ironed, jet-black hair. She's wearing a semi-transparent grey cotton dress. It is very lacy, very short.

Fabrizio grins at her, so I smile too. Her legs are encased in thigh-high leather boots. Thick makeup and heavy gold jewellery top off the outfit. Fabrizio stands, turns to greet her, kissing her on the lips, placing, I note, one hand on her buttocks.

He introduces me. "Rosa, Mark."

Wide-eyed, I shake her hand. As we shake she licks her lips and very slowly, quite deliberately, she winks at me. A waft of cheap perfume whacks me in the face.

I look back at Fabrizio questioningly; I am confused.

He too winks at me, grins and raises his eyebrows silently forming a question. I look between their grinning faces.

I shake my head from side to side, silently forming the answer.

As I walk away I remember the cute sax player, but he's long gone.

Words Fail

The disco spotlights roll across an empty dance floor.

I grimace. "Yves!" I say. "It's completely empty!"

He grabs my arm, steers me to the bar. "I know, I know, it'll fill up."

You can ring my bell is belting from the sound system. "Gee, I haven't heard that one in a while," I say.

"Gin and tonic?" he asks me.

I nod; he orders the drinks.

"Look, if it hasn't livened up by the time he gets here we can just go somewhere else, OK?" he says.

I nod again. "But why *here* anyway?"

Yves shrugs. "Robert likes it; you'll like him, he's so lovely... I can't wait for you to meet, by far the best I've ever had – I think I may marry him!"

"And let's face it Yves, you've had a few." I wiggle my eyebrows at him.

"Yes, well remember, as far as Robert is concerned, I'm a complete virgin."

He hands me my drink. "Yeah, yeah," I say.

People drift into the club. A few freestylers occupy the dance floor. The music is moving through the eighties, they're playing *I'm so excited*. I start to move my shoulders to the rhythm as I sip at my drink.

Yves is swinging his hips; I can tell he wants to dance. He plonks his drink down, grabs my arm. "Come on, I love this," he says.

Hand on your heart is starting. I hate Kylie, especially the old stuff from the Stock Aitken Waterman days. "Nearly into the nineties!" I shout.

Yves grins wildly, flails his arms around like someone who has never thought about how he looks, or never got to dance to this stuff first time around, never learnt how to do it properly or even better not to do it at all. I'm embarrassed, but the dance floor fills, slowly cramping his style.

They play *Pump Up The Jam*. I actually start to enjoy myself, groove my hips to the music. I close my eyes to shut out the people standing around the edge of the dance floor and to shut out the grotesque image of Yves dancing with himself in front of a mirror.

Suddenly he grabs my arm and I open my eyes. In front of me, immobile in the midst of the flashing and the twirling is a man. He has clipped brown hair, impossibly blue, almost turquoise eyes, a half smile spread across his lips. He's unshaven and he's smiling at me.

It seems that the world around us has stopped, or maybe that the world around continues to swirl and swing and flash, but I, and he, and the space between us has stopped.

My heart is pumping, pulsing blood through my veins at triple speed. I actually worry for a split second that this is the start of a heart attack.

The man leans in to kiss me on the cheek; the contact is electric, incredible, ecstatic. We stare at each other, amazed.

"Robert," says Yves. "Meet my friend Mark."

Goose bumps spread across my arms as we stare at each other.

"Hi!" I say as nonchalantly as I can manage.

"Hello," he says. His voice lifts almost imperceptibly at the end, but I hear it.

I look at Yves, who is grinning at me. "Isn't he lovely?" he asks.

I nod. Speechless. "I'll erm, go get a drink, I think..." I stammer.

Yves hasn't heard me over the music, so I point to the bar and lift an imaginary drink to my lips.

As I watch them from the bar, my heartbeat slows to a normal rhythm. I drink another gin and tonic even though I shouldn't; I have to drive home, but I need it.

Yves is clowning around on the dance floor, imitating John Travolta. Robert looks embarrassed, he's dancing with his eyes closed, grooving sedately. He glances over at me and grins, raising an eyebrow. I smile back.

Yves grabs him from the side, pulls him in, kisses him. I go to the toilet.

On the way back I meet Yves going in. "Isn't he lovely?" he asks again.

I nod, "Yeah, he's really cute."

"And intelligent. I'm in *love,*" he confides with a little nod.

I dance a little but the dance floor has become crowded. When I brush against Robert, he stares into my eyes with a little too much intensity, so I head back to the bar where I smoke and drink Coke instead.

As we leave, Robert lays an arm around my waist. "Yves said maybe you could drop me off," he says.

I wriggle free and look to Yves for confirmation. "I'm working at six tomorrow," he says, shrugging. "Robert lives right on your route."

I wince; I nod. "Yeah, sure," I say through gritted teeth.

On the street corner, Yves kisses Robert goodbye.

There is a deathly silence between us. Robert tap taps his fingers on the top of the glove compartment as I drive along the empty three lanes of the Promenade des Anglais. "So how long have you known Yves?" he asks.

I laugh, "Oh forever – maybe four years. He was the first person I met here."

He nods. "He's nice," he says. "Were you two ever...?"

I laugh. "No, never. He really likes *you* though."

Robert laughs.

I change down, start to slow for the traffic lights, glance sideways at him. "What?" I ask.

"Oh, it's just that it'll never work out between me and Yves," he says.

I swallow and pull up at the lights. "Why? You said you liked him."

Robert coughs. "Oh I do, but Yves is just after something cool, you know, no commitment, no complications, he's like that," he says. "I'm different really, and well, actually, I really like *you.*"

I breathe out heavily; I scratch my ear. My heart starts to pound again, I can feel him looking at me and I wish the lights would change. When he slides a hand onto my thigh, I roll my head, sigh and push his hand away.

"Sorry," he says.

"It's just, I mean you *are* going out with my friend," I say. "And Yves always *says* he just wants something cool, but..."

"You can go," says Robert.

I look at him uncomprehendingly.

He nods at the lights. "It's green, you can go..."

"Oh, yeah," I say, pulling away.

He puts his hand back on my leg. "But I don't love Yves," he says, "and I do really like you."

I shake my head. "I can't," I say. "I can't do that to Yves. I'm sorry. Maybe another time, another place..."

Robert pulls his hand back. "Yves is a wanker. He doesn't know *what* he wants," he says.

I stare at the road. *Je t'aime moi non plus* is playing on the radio, Jane Birkin is grunting and groaning.

"Yeah, well, I just happen to *like* that wanker," I say.

I swing around the corner, head down to the port.

"You can drop me here," says Robert.

"Sure, where abouts do you live?"

"You can drop me here," he repeats coldly.

I pull in, lightly bumping the kerb.

Robert gets out of the car, then leans back in. He grabs my head, kisses me lightly on the lips. "See you around," he says.

I watch him walk away. I actually open my mouth; actually start to breathe his name to call him back. But I don't.

Chic Girls

I push through the door into the bar, my coat over my head against the rain. "My God!" I exclaim as I remove the coat. Madonna is thumping out of the sound system. "I haven't seen rain like that for a while," I add, glancing around – the room is empty.

A single guy sits at the bar, the barman is handing him a beer. He grins at me. "Nice weather huh?" he says.

I hang up my wet coat and wipe the drips from my forehead with my sleeve. I pull my cigarettes from my pocket; pull a stool up next to the other client. He's smallish, delicate build – maybe one metre seventy-five. Brown hair, little round glasses, black trousers, and a white shirt – cute in a compact kind of a way.

"Jesus it's quiet," I say looking around the emptiness of the bar.

Gilles nods. "The rain," he says morosely.

The guy next to me clears his throat. "It's not the quantity that counts, it's the quality," he says. He has an unusual accent I can't place. He doesn't sound French.

I smile at him. "True enough," I say.

"Gilles! A beer for my friend," he says.

Gilles nods, pulls another bottle of Stella from the fridge, and in a single elegant movement uncaps it, swings it onto the bar and lifts away an empty bottle.

"I said it's not the quantity that counts," the man repeats. "It's the quality." He sounds a little drunk.

I grin at Gilles, raise an eyebrow. "Yeah. You're quite right," I say.

"English?" asks the man, "or American?"

"English," I say. I pull a magazine towards me across the counter and start to flick through it.

"English is good," he says. "I like English."

I glance at him. "Thanks," I say. I look back at the magazine, turn the pages over. It's really too dark in here to be able to read any of the small text but I pretend.

"My ex-boyfriend was English," he says. He leans in towards me conspiratorially, glances back at Gilles, then continues, "he had a huge dick."

I frown; I nod. "That's nice," I say.

"Michael, leave the man alone," Gilles tells him.

He sits up straight. "I met him in Zurich," he continues. "I'm Swiss." He places a hand on my leg.

I move my knee and his hand falls to his side. "So, you live here?" he asks me.

I nod. "Yes," I say.

"Thass good," he slurs, nodding at me and staring blankly.

I sigh.

"Another beer?" he asks.

I shake my head. "Nah, you're OK thanks." I wave the bottle at him to indicate that it is still full.

He leans on the bar then back towards me again. "I like the English," he says again.

I smother a laugh. "I know," I say. "Thanks. You said."

I look over at Gilles. "Do you think it will fill up?" I ask him.

He shrugs. "Only if the rain stops," he says.

"Gissanother beer," says Michael.

Gilles leans, looks into his eyes. "You sure?" he asks. "You seem to be sinking them at one hell of a rate."

The man nods. His mouth pouts. "Iss a bar isn't it? Anyway I wanna get pissed," he says.

As Gilles turns to the fridge behind him and reaches up for another bottle of beer, the door to the bar opens behind me.

I turn to look. A man enters; early thirties – blond, fit. He's wearing a white t-shirt; it says: *I'm not gay but my boyfriend is.* It's soaked; it sticks to his torso. Rain drips from his hair, which he pushes from his eyes as he crosses the bar towards us.

Gilles glances at him. "Just in time," he says under his breath.

The man's face is red; his eyes are too. For some reason, I stand. I put my beer down on the counter and take a step back; it's automatic, instinctive.

The man moves between Michael and myself.

Gilles turns, says, "Hi th..." He pauses mid sentence.

For maybe half a second no one moves, but then, before I can begin to understand what is happening, Gilles starts to run to the end of the bar, to the opening. As he runs he shouts, "Christophe! Non!"

My mouth falls into a silent *no.* I see the back of the man's head recoil, then thrust forwards. I hear a sickening crunch.

Michael's glasses fly through the air and land at my feet. His head lurches backwards. He staggers, his nose already sprouting jets of red, staining his white shirt. He falls against a barstool and Gilles catches him from behind.

Christophe turns, still dripping, towards *me.* "Fils de pute!" he says. – *Son of a bitch.*

I frown at him; my eyes burn with outrage. "What?" I spit.

We glare at each other for half a second. Instinctively I remove my own glasses, place them on the bar.

He glares at them, glares back at me.

Gilles starts to speak, "Christophe, you can't just..." but he's already heading for the door.

He turns back briefly to face Michael. "Salope!" he shouts. – *Slut.* The door swings closed behind him.

Gilles lifts Michael to his feet and nods calmly towards the door. "Can you lock it?" he asks me. "In case he comes back."

But Michael wobbles on his feet, one hand on the bar, the other holding his bloodied nose. "No," he says walking slowly towards the door, "I have to go." I reach down, grab his glasses before he walks on them, and hand them to him.

He pushes the door open – the rain is falling in white illuminated sheets. A channel of water gushes from an overflowing gutter to the right of the entrance. He pauses momentarily, looking back at me – still holding his nose. "Snice to meet you," he says. "Au revoir."

The door swings closed behind him.

I turn to Gilles. "D'you still want me to lock it?" I ask.

"No, not now," he says, reaching over behind the bar to grab some kitchen roll.

I shake my head and open my mouth, searching for words.

Gilles crouches down and starts to mop up the blood specks.

"What the fuck was all that about?" I ask.

Gilles snorts, sighs, shrugs, and shakes his head. "They take it in turns," he says. "It's what they do."

"What, beat each other up?"

He nods his head from side to side to mean *sort of.* "Cheating on each other, getting drunk, beating each other up... that kind of stuff."

I raise a hand to my nose. I wince. "Nice," I say. "Real nice."

"Et oui, ce sont des filles très chic," says Gilles. – *Yes, they're very chic girls.*

Madonna is still singing.

Guy

I bend my knees the way I was taught, lift the box from the floor, heave it onto my shoulder, and start tremblingly up the stairs. Sweat trickles down my face, my arm, my neck. *"Why would anyone move in August?"* I wonder.

I look at the guy in front of me carrying one end of Yves' sofa. My eyes are level with his arse; he's wearing tight, faded jeans. "God, I feel so butch!" he laughs.

When the lorry is empty he says, "I'll drive you back if you want. I drive right past anyway."

I hesitate.

"Get in," he says.

His name is Guy; he talks constantly. "I intend to be living with someone by January," he tells me. "Are you single?"

A single light flashes on a console somewhere deep down. It says, "Run away! Evacuate!"

I don't know why, maybe too many evenings watching T.V. alone, but I choose to ignore it and swap phone numbers.

Monday he phones to ask me to dinner. I say I'm busy and end up feeling bored and depressed in front of the T.V. again.

Tuesday when he phones to ask me to the cinema, I say, "Yes."

I want to see *High Heels*, the latest Almodovar film; Guy wants to see *Notting Hill*. We watch *Notting Hill*. The warning light flashes faster.

He phones me on Saturday Morning. We wander around Nice Etoile together. He seems to know a shop assistant in every store. I listen to the chitchat and feel my feet ache.

We buy CDs at the FNAC – I buy Nitin Sawhney, Guy buys Celine Dion.

I resist sleeping with him or even situations where it might happen – for a while. We meet in cinemas and restaurants and bars, I want to be sure about something, sure that there is at least some point to it, and I'm not at all sure that there is.

My friend Yves raises an eyebrow. "If you want to be sure, then shag him," he says. "Then you'll know right away."

Two weeks later with a couple of drinks down the hatch, it happens. Guy covers me with slobbery kisses; afterwards he says, "I love you."

It's all wrong, and I know this – the warning lights are accompanied by a small siren. So why am I doing this?

He invites me to dinner, and I meet his friends. They're all women and strangely, without exception are shop assistants. He defrosts the sauce, pours it over the pasta, and serves it on flowered plates.

I watch him being camp and pretentious, showing me off in front of them; I wonder what I'm doing here.

Guy kisses my head each time he walks past. He's always buzzing, always talking. I find myself zoning out, unable to listen to the word-by-word, act-by-act, argument-by-argument story of his day, but slowly, surely, I get used to it. At least it doesn't feel so empty when he's around.

He meets my friend Isabelle. "What the hell are you doing with him?" she asks.

"I don't know," I say honestly. And it's true, I don't. Even so, I feel angry with her for not liking him.

In October, Guy says, "I want more, I want us to live together."
I say, "No way."
"If you loved me you would," he says. "It's all or nothing."
I try to bluff. I say, "OK then. Nothing."
So we split up.

I spend a week sitting alone in my apartment eating dinner with my cat. My heart's not broken; I know that. But I miss him all the same.

"Maybe I am in love," I think. Maybe I just don't want to admit it. *And how come the bastard doesn't call anyway?*

I wish I had two lives, so that in one I could go back to Guy, whilst in the other I would give up. At the moment of my death I'd compare the two and see which one worked out best.

I know it's not right, but I choose to move in with him.

I see myself from the outside; feel detached from my own actions. I watch this Mark character in surprise and I don't understand what he's doing any more.

I watch him miserably pack up boxes, shift them out, move them in. I see him negotiating the mixing and matching of furniture.

I keep thinking, *"Why are you doing this?"* – I carry on anyway.

Sometimes it's OK, sometimes it's good. He's not a *bad* man.

Sometimes he's sad and I empathise, then I momentarily connect to him – *"Maybe I do love him after all,"* I think.

It's just that there's so little man to love, so much of his character that is superficial cliché, all cynicism and retail-queen attitude. The substance of him flakes away the more you chip at it. His opinions can change on any subject within the hour, and then change back again; it just depends who he most wants to agree with.

I hang on to the old apartment for three months. There is no logic to it, but I just don't get around to dealing with it. I'm very busy, very stressed with my job. That's my excuse anyway.

Guy knows. He says, "It's empty, get rid of it."

I say, "I just don't feel ready."

He says, "If you loved me you would."

He says, "Maybe you should just move back out if that's how you feel."

I consider it for another month, a month of sulking and arguments, a month of dreading coming home and dreading having to discuss it again, then I hand back the keys.

"Are you sure about this?" asks the man from the agency, looking into my eyes.

I shrug, say nothing and walk away.

"I've been offered that job in the States," I tell him one evening.

It's a week after our first anniversary. I didn't have the heart to mention it a week ago when they told me.

Guy pauses, a forked prawn halfway to his mouth – it drops back to Earth. "You're not *thinking* about it are you?" he asks. "You wouldn't."

The weather forecast is there for all to see, storms brewing. I laugh. "No," I say, staring at my plate.

I marvel at my own weakness. *What has happened to me?*

Guy sulks for a week anyway.

We look through holiday catalogues, but none of the holidays appeal to me, I really just want to go travelling in a camper van.

"You'll like it," Guy insists. "It's just what you need. The perfect anti-stress: palm trees, beaches..."

I imagine the sea lapping at my feet. I look at the man in the picture, sipping a cocktail at a beach bar.

"Maybe he's right," I tell Isabelle. "Maybe it *is* what I need."

She looks at me as if I am an alien. "Whatever," she says.

We book it; I pay. It's the most expensive holiday I have ever had.

But I hadn't imagined the trilingual Italian DJ. I hadn't imagined the shared breakfast tables, the children's disco, the jugglers, the clowns or the Club-Med representative prodding me awake as I doze on the beach, prodding me to tell me that I'm missing all the fun.

I wander up to the pool, to see what exactly the fun is.

Guy is there – I see him lined up with everyone else. Everyone is drunk, everyone is pink and sunburnt – a couple of hundred people in a circle around the pool.

Euro-disco is blaring from the speakers – a Swedish sounding girl-star with a horrible high voice singing a Madonna song.

The Italian DJ is on a platform overhanging the pool. He's moving his hands to the right, moving his hands to the left – he's shimmying and rubbing his arse.

They copy him: the fat middle-aged women, the wiry old men, the six year olds, the blonde Essex girls, Guy...

I look at him uncomprehendingly as he wiggles his fingers above his head, his face distorted with childlike joy.

I am frozen, I cannot move – the flashing light becomes a whole panel of flashing lights, a stream of roaring, screaming sirens, and they have all been there forever, except suddenly now, I hear them. They fill my head and I know what they mean.

"And ready, and one two three *spin!*" shouts the DJ.

As Guy spins he catches sight of me, smiles broadly and beckons me in.

I force a smile and as I wander away the sound fades behind me. The man on the beach tells me again that I am missing all the fun.

"Fuck off," I tell him.

"Why didn't you come?" asks Guy over dinner.

I tell him that I hate it, that I can't think of anything worse.

He says, "You'd have such a good time, come tomorrow?"

I shake my head.

"Just try? For me?" he says. "If you loved..."

I shake my head. I interrupt him. "I'm sorry, we're very different. I hate it, I think it's bollocks. I think it's the worst holiday experience imaginable," I say.

His face falls. He eats in silence for a while. "You're so uptight," he says, finally.

"Not uptight," I say, "just different." But in a way I think he's right. Even if I did want to get up there and dance, I couldn't. I'm too reserved. *"Too worried about looking stupid,"* I think. Too aware that I *would* look stupid.

"Well, if that's the way you feel," he says.

"Look, does it matter?" I ask. "I mean why do we have to agree on absolutely everything?"

He looks sullen; he pushes his plate away. "You have to spoil it," he says. "I haven't had such a good time since..."

"I know," I say.

He stares at me. "We never have any fun together," he says.

"I know," I say.

"I'm sick of it," he says. "I'm sick of you. I want more, and if you can't give it then maybe..."

"I know," I say. "Look, I've been thinking... About that job in New York..."

Julian Barclay

We first chat via Compuserve, the proprietary pre-Internet email and chat service. My company is sending me to New York for six months and though I'm happy to escape; I'm scared: New York equals death on the streets, the sound of gunshot, police sirens that wake you up in the night. It's also a place where I don't know a soul, not one contact.

I decide to post an ad in a New York gay forum and see if anyone wants to befriend me. Julian Barclay is the first to answer my ad.

He replies immediately and the following messages show an openness that astounds me. He's a warehouse manager; he lives with his boyfriend, Bill. They're bikers, he'd be happy to show me around.

After a week or so I have received other replies but they are all either weird, or as the Americans would say, after my ass. I'm quite scared enough as it is.

Julian and I exchange a few more emails before I leave. He lives on Long Island, they have a big place; I must go and visit sometime.

My own apartment turns out to be tiny, hugely expensive (for my company) but very central Manhattan, thirty-seventh and sixth.

On the second day, I call Julian from my new phone. I hear his voice on the answer-phone for the first time. It is rich and masculine. He calls me back around eleven-thirty p.m. – I've just got into bed. I tell him this and he asks if I am naked and laughs.

He invites me for breakfast the next morning, explains how to get to Union square; he sounds funny, clever, relaxed. When I hang up, I drift off to sleep imagining him and listening to the distant police sirens.

The coffee shop is exactly as a coffee shop should be. A long Formica counter top, chrome swivel bar stools, a girl chewing gum with an order book pushed into the belt of her apron. Like much of America it is standard film cliché and as such it feels instantly familiar to just about anyone.

A hand waves from a booth at the rear of the bar, it is Julian – he's smiling. His crash helmet is on the tabletop.

I cross the bar nervously. He smiles broadly, shakes my hand firmly, says, "Mark! Hello!"

He's a big guy, maybe one metre eighty-five, no doubt a swimmer or a regular gym goer.

He's wearing leather motorcycle pants and thick biceps bulge from the sleeves of his grey t-shirt. His stubble is longer than his haircut.

He bangs the table. "Well sit down!" he says.

As I slide in behind the table, he stares at me. There seems to be laughter in his eyes. The effect on me is unexpected and immediate; I am aroused. I shuffle my feet under the table.

Breakfast goes well. We talk about my job, about New York, about motorbikes. He tells me about his parents, his brothers and sisters, nothing seems taboo. I will find out that for New Yorkers virtually nothing *is* taboo, but for now it simply strikes me that this man is exceptionally honest and open.

I am quite under his manly spell when he says, "I'm afraid I can't on Friday, I have a GMSM meeting."

I sip my coffee, chew on a pancake. Something registers but it remains subconscious for the moment. "How about Saturday?" I ask.

Julian shakes his head, "Parents for dinner, maybe Sunday? Unless you want to come with us on Friday..."

I stop chewing. "What did you say? A *what* meeting?"

Julian signals to the waitress for more coffee. As she swings by to fill his cup he says, "GMSM, the Gay Men's Sado Maso Group."

The waitress offers me coffee and moves on without flinching.

He peers into my eyes. "Hello! Is anybody there?"

I laugh. "Sure, just taking in new information..."

Didn't I mention that to you in my mails? I was sure I did..."

I shake my head. "No, but it doesn't matter, what happens at GMSM meetings? Dare I ask?"

Julian forks bacon into his mouth. "Oh it's cool," he says. "It's in like a really big bar, and there are, you know, slaves and masters, and spectators..."

"What happens to the slaves, I mean, what do the spectators watch?"

"It's a dungeon demo, so they're like tied to the wall or whatever, and there are demonstrations of all the different SM techniques."

I nod and try to do this knowingly. "Like?" I say.

"Like hot-wax and tit-torture, bondage... Everything really. You should come, you don't have to participate in anything you don't want to."

I stare at my plate and cough. I smirk slightly. "I don't think..."

Julian touches my hand. "Oh of course if you want to participate, if you want to be..." he looks into my eyes questioningly. "A slave... or whatever, then you can, you just tell them what you like; it's all very safe and controlled."

An image flashes through my head. I am chained to the wall, I am blindfolded, people unknown, are playing with my body, pulling on my nipples, playing with my arse... I shake my head. I laugh.

"I'm afraid I'm not really into SM," I say. My dick throbs and I hear the lie. I realise something consciously for the first time in my life; that I could be, if I let myself.

Julian forks a potato and points it at me. "You need to let go, you need to just let it happen."

"But do I?" I wonder. I smile. "I think you've got the wrong end of the stick."

He puts down his fork, grabs my hand and looks into my eyes again. "Have I?"

I stare him out, I nod, I lie. I say, "Yes."

Julian waves over the waitress, asks her for the check, stands. "Let's go for a walk," he says.

I'm embarrassed, I still have a hard-on, but I stand and follow him holding my bomber jacket in front. He slides his hand across my arse, pushes me out into the cold October air. We pull on our jackets; he's beautiful, glistening in his black leathers. He has a chrome ring clipped to his shoulder epaulet. I feel childlike in front of him.

He says, "This way."

We turn and start to walk down the road; he slides a hand into my back pocket. I let it remain for a while, then pull away.

He stops, turns to face me, looks at me questioningly. He says, "I know what I forgot."

I raise an eyebrow. "What?"

"I didn't welcome you to New York." With this he places his crash helmet on the newspaper distributor beside him, wraps an arm behind my back and kisses me, forcing his tongue into my mouth.

He crushes me towards him, then pulls away, looks into my eyes and reaches inside my jacket to pinch my nipple, grinning as I gasp. "If you're not ready for the Dungeon Demo, you could come out and visit us at our place," he says. "We have a fully equipped playroom... we could give you a nice, soft introduction. Just whatever you want to try."

I run a hand across his jacket, down over his back pocket.

I have three thoughts simultaneously: that no offer has ever excited me more, that it is quite a big surprise that this excites me so, and that I am heading onto dangerous ground, very dangerous ground. I could actually end up dying in some basement somewhere or, be held captive in a cage for years. *"Hey, I've seen pulp fiction,"* I think.

Finally, I think that even if I don't get hurt in the process, even if it all goes "fine", that I may never get out of this thing again, that it could be like tasting heroin – *the first one*, as the dealers say, *is free.*

I pull away, but this time there is decision in the movement. Julian lets go of me, stands back, smiles at me. He picks up his crash helmet, pulls his keys from his pocket.

"If you decide you want to try something, or even if you just want to talk about it, you have my number..."

I nod; I shrug. "Sorry," I say.

Julian shrugs. "You'll get over it, and when you do, well you know where I am." With this he turns and walks away, shooting me a wink as he rounds the corner.

I think about calling Julian Barclay every day that I stay in New York – that's at least once a day for six months.

Sometimes, even now, I think I should have called him. Sometimes I think that I still might. But I never do, I just never have the nerve.

Blow

He smiles. "Hi! How are you?" he says. I look at him and wonder if I know him. He is clean-cut, tall, thin, fit – short blond hair, blue eyes peering through oval Armani glasses. The light in the bar is low. I feel fairly sure that I don't. "Sorry, I don't think we've..."

He holds out a hand. "Brian." His smile bares long, white-capped, all-American dentistry.

"Mark." I shake his hand.

"So Mark. Where are you from? You sound British."

I scan the man's clothes as I reply, expensive grey suit, white shirt, double cuffs, and discreet grey tie. "I am, well originally from the south-east of England, then France, and now here."

"Oh, you live here. Cool! Manhattan?"

"Yeah, thirty-seventh and sixth."

"Nice address, how many square feet do you have there?"

I frown. This is starting to sound like a marketing survey. "Um, don't know really, it's a small two-room apartment."

Brian nods. "A brownstone?"

I smile. "Yes, do you work in real estate or something?"

Brian frowns. "No why?"

I shrug. "You just seem interested in where I live, that's all."

Brian raises the palms of his hands. "Hey man, just making conversation."

I have offended him, and I guess that this is simply yet another culture gap to be bridged. "Sorry, I guess people aren't so inquisitive in the UK."

Brian visibly relaxes. "So what do they talk about in the UK?"

I shrug again. "Don't know really, normal stuff I suppose, the weather, clothes, music..."

"OK let's try again," says Brian. "Nice suit you have there, very smart."

I smile. "I was thinking the same thing about you. You work near here?"

Brian opens his eyes wide and cocks his head to one side. "Hey now who's the inquisitive one?"

"I haven't seen you here before, that's all."

"Oh, I often call in for a drink, mainly Fridays though." He reaches out and strokes my lapel. "Very nice though, is that an Armani?"

I laugh. The suit is from Marks and Spencer's.

Brian appears vexed. "Hey what is it with you? What *do* you want to talk about?"

I shrug. "Sorry," I say.

"If you prefer," he continues, "we could talk about you coming back to my place, and me blowing you."

I can feel myself reddening and glance around to see if anyone is listening, but everyone nearby is seemingly engrossed in their own conversations.

"That's pretty, um, direct Brian."

"Sure. I love to blow a man in a suit, and you don't seem to like the small-talk so..." he grins. "What the hell."

I smile. "Yeah, what the hell."

"So?"

"What? *Now?*"

"Sure, now."

The situation is absurd. We have talked real estate for ten minutes, and here he is inviting me to his place for oral sex, but I want to do it. I swig at my beer raking through my thoughts to get a handle on my motivation.

He's very cute, self-assured, well dressed, and sexy in a rather bland, lawyer kind of a way. The offer is obscene and yet naive at the same time, almost childlike, as if coming from a space I had once known, a space where none of this stuff was meant to be bad or dirty.

Of course the only time that none of this was bad or dirty was before I even knew that it existed, but all the same. I feel an urge to accept precisely because this is so entirely un-me, to go back with someone for sex, at nine p.m. on a Friday evening, after ten minutes of polite chat.

It seems ridiculous and story-like, and I feel driven to experience something different, something that someone else would do, probably someone in a film I know, but as the man says, what the hell? At least it doesn't sound as dangerous as visiting Julian Barclay.

"Sure," I say.

Brian has been looking concerned. He punches my arm. "Good!"

His apartment is a short taxi ride away; during the journey he stares from his window in silence. I doubt my reason, sift through the possibilities that he's a sadist or serial killer, but just as I am plucking up courage to stop the cab, to jump out, we have arrived, and he's leading me past the doorman. "He's with me," he says, taking me on into the elevator.

It is not until we have stepped into his apartment that he speaks again. "Hang up your coat," he says pulling his own coat and jacket off. He's wearing grey silk braces; they match his tie.

I start to undress too but Brian stops me. "No keep the suit, just take off your overcoat."

I do as he requests. He pushes me against the closed apartment door, kneels before me, pulls at my zip, pulls my dick from my trousers and immediately slips it into his mouth. I smile, amazed and disconcerted.

Brian pumps away, reaching up, pinching my nipples through my shirt. I try to stroke his head, to unzip his own trousers, to kiss him, but he refuses any involvement on my part. I resign myself – it isn't so bad.

When I come, Brian flops my dick back into my trousers and stands up. He grins broadly. "Thanks," he says pulling me towards him.

For an instant I think that he will kiss me, I imagine that it is now his turn, but he just wants to open the door behind me.

He hands me my coat – I am dazed. He grips my shoulders, spins me around and points me towards the corridor. "This is where we say goodbye," he says.

As the door closes behind me I start to laugh.

Clueless

We meet in Champs, a large, smooth, disco-bar. It's three times the size of the biggest bar I ever visited in France. I am standing watching others watch the sterile, body-perfect go-go dancer. Everyone is drinking *Bud*. Disco lights swing across my face blinding me in time with the beat.

A voice says, "Hello." The man holds out a hand. "Darren."

"Excuse me," he says. "But could I ask you what you do for a living, because I have a bet with my friend. He says you're in TV and I say you're some kind of an artist."

I tell Darren I'm setting up a branch office for a French company.

He says, "Oh." He looks disappointed.

I add, "But I do write in my spare time."

He grins. "Wait. I'll get my friend Henry."

They form a comedy double act. Darren talks a lot, it's like having a personal TV channel – he's witty, fast, funny. He kind of sounds like the guy in the American sitcoms, you know, the funny one, the one who thinks of all the great put-downs on the spur of the moment instead of the next day like real people do. Henry is his stooge – he gently smiles as he's ragged to death. Though Darren is sharper, I like Henry best.

I tell them that I have only been in New York for two weeks. "I don't really know anyone yet," I say.

"Oh my God!" exclaims Darren. "It's just like Clueless!"

"You will be Tai," he tells me, "the new girl in school."

"I'll be Cher, and..." he prods Henry in the stomach, "you can be Diane."

They laugh at their new project; they'll teach me the ropes, tell me what to do, where to go, how to be.

"What to wear is easy," says Henry. "This is New York, so just wear black." I note that virtually everyone *is* wearing black and make a mental note to go shopping.

I laugh. I say, "I've never seen, what's it called?" They agree that seeing Clueless will be the first part of my education.

And a new life it turns out to be, an amazing stroke of luck.

My lonely New York outsider life changes overnight to a frantic social whirl of restaurants, dinner-parties with caterers (*no-one* cooks) and guided tours of New York nightlife.

Darren leads, organises, buzzes around. He talks and talks and we laugh appreciatively.

Henry watches, Henry listens, and when Darren is not around Henry tells me he has cancer. He tells me of his treatment, tells me that he has no time for assholes anymore.

He starts to tell me about his English aunt, but then he stops suddenly and says, "Anyway enough of me, let's talk about you."

I am thrown – he was in full flow. I pause. I say, "Erm..."

Henry shakes his head and rolls his eyes. "OK, well! Enough of you then, let's talk about *me* again!" he says.

He tells me he's in remission, says he grew up in the same precinct as Darren. They had the same model of house, a "Sheffield."

"I lived in the Cs, Carol Crescent, between Chrysanthemum Drive and Cheryl Close," he tells me. "Darren lived in the B's. Benjamin drive," he says. "The Bs were so much more where-it-was-at, so Darren got to grow up feeling all *superior* you know?"

I start a new diary. *"Darren is so funny, I just love him. But Henry, Henry is special,"* I write.

I'm not sure really what I think about him. It's a new kind of relationship for me – uncharted emotional territory – but he's sinking into my skin, worming his way through the layers of British reserve.

"You British are so slow!" he exclaims, clicking his fingers. "Wake up! Wake up!"

But he learns to give me the time to express myself and I tell him about the death of my father; we compare notes on our failed relationships.

In coffee shops throughout Manhattan and walking around Union Square market on cold winter mornings, while driving to Long Island, another part of my "education," we exchange and swap stories. Slowly, over the months, our auras merge.

I don't think Henry realises what's happening, I certainly don't.

We don't know what's happened until the end.

Friends Forever

We are sitting on the sofa. We've been out to *The Bar* and we're drunk. I hate my job, and I can't stay here without it, and though I love New Yorkers, I hate New York. I had thought it would be the other way around. I can't live somewhere where even when the sun *does* shine you don't get to see it – I can't live in the shade of these buildings any longer.

Henry is looking into my eyes. I've only known him for five months, but I know the door to his soul is as wide open as I have ever come across, and I've been in, looked around and liked what I've seen.

He says, "Are you sure you've thought about this?"

I can hear him slurring, as drunk as myself.

I nod. "I've thought of nothing else for the last month."

"Because I don't think..." His eyes gleam, his voice shudders. "I actually don't want you to leave," he says.

My own eyes water. I stroke his hair. I say, "I know."

He leans in towards me, his head fits comfortably on my shoulder. I stroke his back.

"I think I love you," he says.

"I know. I think I love you as well," I say.

My dick is stirring, surprise! I had never thought of Henry sexually before, not once. He sits back, stares into my eyes for maybe a minute.

I am torn; torn between a physical law, something to do with magnetic attraction of close bodies, a desire for fusion with all that is loved, and logic – this can go nowhere, this can only hurt, it is futile, I am going back to France. I know that Henry must be a brother, not a lover.

We brush lips, we kiss, gently, then in unison we stop, we pull back.

I shudder, another tear. "Life's not fair," I say.

Henry laughs, swallows hard. "It's bullshit isn't it?" he says. He smiles at me, starts to shine, to radiate. It's not the first time I've seen him do this. "It's OK though," he says. His eyes are astoundingly beautiful.

I look at him questioningly. He shrugs. "We don't have to live together, we can't live with *everyone* we love."

I frown.

"We love so many people." He speaks calmly, as if in a trance. "Friends, lovers, family, ex boyfriends... We can't live with them all."

I nod.

"But it doesn't matter..."

He moves back onto the sofa, rests his head back on my shoulder. "Only the love matters. It doesn't matter if it's on the other side of the world."

I have a feeling I am letting slip away the kindest man I've ever met.

"Don't worry," he says. "We'll always be friends, our whole lives."

I slide an arm around his shoulder.

"We will," I say.

Sell By Date

I sit nodding, listening. The conversation is the same one as last time, the same as the one before I left, seven months ago. Only the names change. The vicious circle of Yves' love life is driving me insane and the fact that his own reactions to it never seem to evolve is bringing me to the point where I am wondering if I can continue to see him, if our friendship hasn't somehow reached its sell-by date.

He's waving a pasta twirl at me. "So you can imagine! I'm left sitting on my own at home like a twat while he sleeps in a hotel less than a mile away rather than come to me! I mean, it's not as if he doesn't know how I feel about him."

I say, "Yes, Yves." I sigh discretely. I imagine him saying, *"Enough of me..."* as Henry used to. *As if.* "Will he ever ask me about New York?" I wonder.

He continues. I stare out through the front of the restaurant. The winter sun is casting hard shadows on the pavement. Strange people are lingering outside the tattoo parlour opposite. I look at my empty plate; I'm still hungry but this is Yves' choice of restaurant, not mine – all big plates and fancy prices, but precious little to eat.

"But Yves," I interrupt him. "It's always the same."

He shrugs. "So they're *all* arseholes."

I sigh. "But you never meet the men you *want* to meet because you're never clear about who it *is* you want to meet or what *kind* of relationship you want."

Yves grins and frowns at me simultaneously. "I am!" he says. "Gilles is perfect, that's the whole point."

I rub the bridge of my nose. "Gilles is a perfect arsehole."

"You haven't met him."

"He's a perfect arsehole who lives with his partner and has two or three affairs going simultaneously of which you are just one."

Yves nods. "Yeah, put like that," he says. "What a bastard!"

I nod. "So he's not perfect at all, *is he?*"

"Yeah, but I mean apart from that."

"What, like, if he was someone different, he'd be perfect?"

Yves nods his head from side to side. "But I couldn't have known," he says.

"Yves. Your ad! I saw it."

"Yeah, so?"

"Well you asked to meet a guy for cool sexy fun at the weekend with no commitment."

He shrugs. "So?"

"So that's what you got, for God's sake. You can't now start wanting him to marry you!"

"I don't, I'm not like you; I don't have a problem with my own company. I don't need a husband, I'm fine on my own."

I open my eyes wide. I nod, I swallow and wait for the "not like you," to pass. "Yeah, well, except that you do," I eventually say in my calmest voice. "Every time you look for something casual, every time you try to snare them, and every time they run a mile."

"You don't listen to me at *all*, do you," he says.

I nod. "Yes I do. Over and over again."

"I wanted something cool, but it was..."

I interrupt, "So amazingly good that you decided you were in love? You see I do listen, and it's not difficult because it's the same story, time after time."

Yves glares at me. "Sorry if I'm boring you," he says.

"You're not," I say. "It's just that until you get a grip and admit what you really want, until you start announcing *that* to the world, then you're going to continue meeting the men you *say* you want to meet instead of the men you *really* want to meet."

"Yeah, well it's pretty boring talking to you as well," he says.

I grimace at him. I say, "Uh?"

"Yeah," he continues, "you're always so busy telling everyone what you think that you don't even care. You're not even interested in *my* problems, I suppose you'd rather talk about *you.*"

I blow through my lips. "OK," I say. "Let's carry this on another day. We're not getting anywhere here."

Yves grunts. "Typical," he says, "just walk away."

I signal to the waiter for the bill. We pay in cash, both desperate to speed to the end of our time together.

As we leave the restaurant, Yves says, "Goodbye." He uses, *"Au-revoir,"* but makes it sound like, *"Adieu."*

I restrain myself from replying in the same tone of voice. "Yes, see you," I say. I start to turn to leave.

"Oh, and Mark?" he says catching my arm. I look back at him, raise my eyebrows, nod. I think, *"Please don't do this."*

"If you're so fucking *clever* on the relationship front," he says, "then how come you're *still single?*"

I stare at him. I search the corners of my brain for a good put-down, but the only thing that comes into my mind is, *Va te faire foutre.* – Go fuck yourself.

So I say, "Good point Yves. Yes. Good point! Thanks for that."

Being Clear

It takes me a few days to write the ad, only seconds to copy and paste it onto the web site. If my theory on being clear about what you want is true then it might just work. I log on to check the appearance of my ad. It sits uncomfortably two entries down from Yves'. He looks much cuter than me. I click on my photo. I re-read it one last time.

This great unfolding novel we call life: the joy, the sadness, the beauty, the ugliness – such an amazing chance, such an incredible stroke of luck, or genius.
To wake up every morning and see the trees and the sunlight.
To be able to stroke the cat and to make toast.
To be able to hear neighbours sawing logs and shout at them about the noise...

I am a man. I am thirty-three and I have a life.
I love it, but I'm sick of doing it alone.
I want someone to share it with. Someone to say, "Yes it is a beautiful day."
Someone to say, "Shut up, mellow out." Someone to say, "Will you cook or shall I?" and, "Please don't make that disgusting green soup again."
Someone to say, "I love you too."
I can see him in my mind. He looks normal, ordinary, except for a glint in the eye, a tendency to smile a lot.
We laugh a lot together. He takes the piss out of me all the time.
We are busy separate entities with different interests and different friends, but when we meet I tell him about the bird I saw in the garden, the accident I nearly had on the motorbike. He tells me of the sad old tramp he saw outside his work place and I read him a phrase from the book I'm currently reading.
And it's all even more beautiful, even more sad, even more poignant, than if we weren't two.
Slowly, surely, we start to decode the mysteries of life together. The power, the amazing, moving, incredibleness of it all becomes even bigger, even more, until our hearts are filled and we think we might explode at the joy of just being able to do it together.
And then of course, we shag.

Drunk and Lonely

I am depressed; I am leaving. The collection of muscle-bound boys, t-shirts swinging from their back pockets, sweating, glistening, as they wobble their perfect pecs across the dance floor does nothing for me tonight. It all seems smooth and superficial and pointless and not what I need.

I miss Henry. Even if the clubs in New York were just as sanitised, we used to have great conversations.

I crave for some real emotion, a real flash of love at first sight, even hate at first sight would do. Some joy, some sadness, instead of this cheap excuse for a good time.

I push through the double doors into the windy winter night and fumble in my pocket for my keys, preparing myself for the drive back to Grasse – alone in the country with my cat and my chickens again.

The cold air bites into my skin and I pull my collar up.

I thought the country would calm me, thought the isolation would be restful, but I just spend my time driving into Nice, and then driving back to the winter desolation of it all.

Sitting on a car bonnet in front of the club is a young lad, maybe twenty-five, maybe even less – at any rate he's around ten years younger than myself.

He has the sultry dark looks that so many seem to have here in the south of France: olive skin, jet-black hair, half-length, swept back from his face, deep brown eyes. He's beautiful; he's drunk. He's wearing a brown leather pilot's jacket and a thick grey scarf wrapped high around his neck; he drunkenly catches my eye and smiles.

I give a crisp grin in return and head towards my car, but I sense him moving, following me.

He grabs my sleeve. "Bonsoir," he says. He sounds like he has a cold.

I turn; he really is *very* beautiful, and *very* drunk.

"Hi," I reply.

"Excuse me?" His speech slurs. "Do you have a car?"

I smile at him nonplussed. I'm jingling my keys in my hand; the car is three meters away. Even if I wanted to, I couldn't deny it. "Sure," I reply. "Why?"

He giggles. He's gripping my arm so tightly it hurts, holding himself upright. "It's just you look nice," he says. – "*Sympa.*"

I roll my eyes upwards and grin, flattered. "You need a lift home?"

He nods. "I'm so drunk... Rue de France."

He wobbles and I hoist his arm around my shoulder and lead him towards the car.

He giggles again. He says, "Oh *bébé!*".

I fumble with the lock with my left hand, and lower him into the passenger seat.

As I drive through the deserted four-am streets he alternates between slumping into momentary sleep – his head lolling forwards – and waking with a start, gripping my thigh.

From time to time I steal a glance at him. He's so very, very beautiful, I think of a line from *Torch Song Trilogy*. *"If he has an IQ of more than ten then there is no God."*

I wonder whether I will take advantage of him. He's keen and drunk, it would be easy.

"Pull up here please," he says, suddenly.

"I thought you said Rue de France," I say stopping the car.

He opens the door and vomits onto the pavement, a brief efficient emptying exercise. I offer him a tissue. He says, "Sorry." He says, "Thank you." We drive on.

When we arrive at his place, I pull up outside but don't park. He undoes his seat belt, then pauses, realising something. He frowns. "Aren't you coming in? I thought you were coming in," he says.

I realise he's asking me, that I couldn't be blamed for accepting, but it just doesn't seem honest – he's that drunk.

"I'm sorry," I say. "I should be getting home, it's nearly five-thirty."

He nods, reaches for the door. My hand hovers on the gear stick.

He pauses, makes a strange, strangled gasp and collapses back into the seat. Tears roll down his cheeks.

I stare at him wide-eyed. I rub my eyes, unsure how to deal with this – he's sobbing now, a deep animal wailing. It's communicating, I too am feeling sad. I touch his shoulder. "What's wrong?"

He explains through the gasps: it's his birthday, he has moved into a new flat today, his stuff is all in boxes, and he can't bear to sleep there alone tonight. "I though I'd found someone," he says.

"It's all a bit heavy," I think.

But I am moved by his sadness, my own eyes are watering in sympathy, so I agree to go in, *"Just for a drink."*

The flat is tiny but newly decorated – it reeks of paint. Sure enough his things are all in boxes, piled against the wall.

On the floor lies a new mattress, still wrapped in plastic, and on an upturned box sits a bottle of whisky and a brimming ashtray.

He sits on the mattress, then sloppily rips the plastic wrapping away. He gestures towards the whisky. "Have a drink," he says as he lies down.

I pour a centimetre of whisky into a cup, and sip at it. He lights a cigarette and I walk through to the kitchen, empty the ashtray and return.

He has closed his eyes; the cigarette is dangling from between his fingertips. His breathing sounds heavy.

I walk to the window and look out at the view of the street; I can see my car. The sky is a deep purple, the first hint of day glimmering in the east.

I hear him snore behind me and turn. I walk over to him, stand over him watching him sleep, then remove the cigarette from his fingertips and crush it in the ashtray.

I sit beside him for a moment, smiling and running my fingers through his shampoo-commercial hair. I wonder how someone so beautiful can end up so sad; I generally think that it all comes down to looks.

He's snoring deeply, his mouth drops open. I pull a business card from my wallet, write, *"Happy Birthday. Call me if you want. Mark."* I push it into his cigarette packet and slip from the door.

Down in the street, a transvestite, a prostitute, asks me if I want to have a good time. I smile at her but shake my head.

In a perfect English accent, she says, "Too bad baby."

As I drive away I realise that I don't even know his name.

I wonder if he will ever call me, and mentally bet that he won't.

Slimming Stripes

I am on the way to the local DIY store when a very good looking man with a little goatee beard stops me and asks me where the... DIY store is. Now I'm a spiritual kind of guy and because I know about chance meetings and destiny and all that kind of stuff, I offer to walk him to the store.

As we walk, he seems to be chatting me up, which is interesting because no one has ever cruised me in the street before (that I've noticed) and because I'm wearing the shorts and shirt I bought with my friend Sylvie yesterday.

Women seem to have some genetically transmitted knowledge about what's flattering or slimming, knowledge which we men, even gay men, somehow missed out on. Sylvie assured me that these shorts give me a, "great arse," and that the vertical stripes on the sides of my surfer shirt are very, "slimming."

Philippe tells me that he works in an art gallery and lives alone nearby. I muse that I should go shopping with Sylvie more often.

Philippe buys a paintbrush, I buy screws and as we leave he asks me back to his apartment to see the *splendide* view. I have a pretty good idea what the view is of, but, well, this *is* destiny after all.

At his flat the moves come thick and fast. When I lean out of the window to appreciate the admittedly impressive though completely inaccessible view, Philippe kisses my neck.

His directness makes me giggle, but when I turn around he shrugs. "I fancy you," he says.

I fancy him too and brazenly kiss him on the lips. We unbutton the amazing slimming shirt.

"Oh," he says stepping back. "I erh... thought you were..."

"What?" I ask, but of course, I know.

"I'm sorry, I thought, you looked ... more ... *defined*," he says.

I shake my head and force a smile. "I'll go," I say.

He protests, half-heartedly, but I leave.

I need to talk to Sylvie.

Saxman

I switch on my Mac. While it starts up I make coffee. I sit with the cup watching the list of messages appear on the screen. "Ahah!" I say out loud. "Finally some replies!" I sip my coffee and click on the first one.

Dear Aladdin.
Nice text. Cute photo. I like bikers.
Here's a picture of me.
Send me a nude pic of yourself if you're interested.
As you can see, the pseudonym is not a joke.
Yours, Doublesize.

The pseudonym is *not* a joke.

Hello Aladdin.
I loved your ad.
I have a very developed sens of humer but don't like fats or fems.
I am ecslusivly pasif in bed.
I curently live in Paris but dont have no objections to coming to live with you in your villa because I don't have a job right now anyway. Please get in touch with me quickly.
Yours, Truelove.

Hi Aladdin.
What a beautiful ad. What a change from "Do you want to suck my dick?"
I'm currently living in Chicago so I can't offer to come and meet you, but I may be moving back next spring; If you like we could keep in touch. I used to live in Nice. I'm thirty-three. I'm a saxophone player. My real name's Steve.
You might even have seen me busking on the Cours Saleya. We used to play there from time to time.
Anyway, right now I'm in Chicago. There's lots of work for jazz musicians here, but I still end up having to give lessons to get by. Story of my life.
I pretty much gave up trying to meet anyone when I reached thirty. I try to fill my life with my music and with friends and adventures, but there's always a little empty hole somewhere deep down. Most of the time I ignore it, but sometimes it hurts.

Sometimes it hurts enough for me to go out to a bar or to have a look at the personal ads. And here I am!
Friends are in their thirties now, they're all getting busy with kids and houses. That doesn't help either I suppose.
I've had a great time here, but I want to move back to France. I'm originally from Toulouse, but I don't know where I'll end up. I still have friends down your way, so who knows...
Anyway, I know that's all a bit vague, but here's a photo of me busking with some friends in front of the Buckingham memorial fountain. The rain came suddenly just afterwards and we got wet and had to move.
I hate motorbikes. Do you like sax? That's sax with an A by the way, not a typo!
Sorry I'm so small in the photo. I don't have anything better.
All the best.
Saxman.

I look at the photo on the screen. I lean in until I can see the individual pixels making it up. Four guys, one girl; all wearing oversize suits, all grinning maniacally. The sax player is balding – he looks like he has dark eyes but it's difficult to tell.

The sax hides his chin. He looks vaguely familiar and I wonder if I ever did see him around.

And then I think, *"Great! Chicago! Brilliant! That's really gonna help!"*

The reply can wait until tomorrow.

Won't Hurt A Bit

He's following me around the bar. I don't like him. I don't like his pot belly or his crooked teeth. I'm flying to Sydney tomorrow morning anyway, off halfway around the world to the world's biggest gay-fest. *"So why am I here again?"* I wonder.

He's wearing a crisp white shirt, and other than the teeth and the belly thing I suppose he's OK. Anyway, he keeps smiling at me.

"Move on; move on," I think, moving away.

I cross to the bar, lean in, kiss the barman on the cheek, order a beer.

A voice to my right says, "I'll have the same please Gilles."

It's a good voice. A baritone voice, intelligent sounding, yet masculine. I turn to look but it's the man with the teeth and the belly. He looks at me, cocks his head on one side, like a chicken. "Bonsoir," he says, holding out a hand. "Ben."

I shake it reluctantly, but it's a good handshake: firm, warm, self assured, the image of his voice. He smiles; his teeth don't look so bad now.

"Must have been the green light at the other end of the bar," I decide.

He stares at me, looks into my eyes a fraction too long. "Bien!" he exclaims, "So you are British Beef? Not mad cow I hope?"

I grin at him. "Vegetarian actually."

He nods, surprised but apparently impressed. "Aha! Vegetarian – not many of those in France!" he says.

We take a table at the rear of the bar, behind the pool table.

Every time I go to the toilets he takes advantage of my absence and buys me another beer. It's a vicious circle, but he makes me laugh and with every beer he looks more attractive.

"I work as a graphic designer," he says. My turn to nod impressed. I like arty people.

"Right now I live on the promenade des Anglais," he says, "but I'm moving to Paris next week, only for six months though."

We discuss Paris, Nice, and possible career options in both.

"I'm flying to Sydney tomorrow," I tell him, "on holiday."

"Tomorrow?" he says. "So can I still fuck you tonight?"

I frown. I feel sure I've heard him wrong over the cheesy techno music.

"I want to undress you, centimetre by centimetre," he says.

I raise an eyebrow.

90

"Then I want to massage you from head to toe," he says. "I'm a *very* good masseur."

I nod. "Is that so?" I say.

"And then I want to lick you all down your spine," he says. "And then, very slowly, very gently, I want to fuck you," he adds, nodding earnestly. He blinks at me, smiles at his own forwardness.

I laugh slightly, embarrassed – the offer is obscene, but right at this moment it sounds like just what the doctor ordered.

He lays a hand on my lap.

I sit there arguing with myself, thinking, *"Why not, what's the harm?"* and *"The guy is quite clearly a complete slut,"* and, *"I'll be really tired on the plane tomorrow,"* and, *"At least I'll sleep during the flight."*

He strokes my thigh. "Your dick says, 'yes,'" he says.

I can't deny that this is exactly what my dick is saying. I give in. "You're on," I say. "It's the best offer I've had all night."

His flat is huge; his bed is placed against huge bay windows overlooking the sea. The atmosphere is pre-storm heavy; in the distance – over the sea towards Corsica – spring storms are already lighting up the sky in little flashes.

Ben is true to his word – it's all very slow, very sensual, very relaxing. Beneath his clothes he's better than I expect, muscular arms, a tight torso, cyclists calves, oh, and a tiny dick, about the size of my index finger. I barely manage to disguise my double take when I look at it.

He massages me from head to toe, slow circular movements, sweet-smelling, amber massage oil. "My brother's a sports masseur," he says. "Taught me everything I know."

I stare at the flashes on the horizon, relax completely beneath the pummelling hands.

"I love to massage," he says quietly.

As I doze, he lies on my back, slithers around on top of me. "I bet your brother didn't teach you that," I murmur.

"No, a Thai," he says.

He pauses, slips on a condom. I glance over my shoulder to make sure he's doing it properly, make sure he's not getting massage oil on it.

"This won't hurt a bit," he says. It doesn't.

It's a surprise though, with no preparation at all – just a little prick as they say at the hospital. But it's fine: it feels warm and intimate, a kind of internal massage.

He continues to slither around on top and inside of me. He pummels my shoulder blades. I wonder if I won't actually fall asleep, wonder vaguely if he would be upset.

"Good?" he asks occasionally.

"Um," I murmur.

He pulls away, I watch him disappear into the kitchen. He returns with a glass of water.

"Sorry," he says, sipping his water and simultaneously sliding a finger into my arse.

I groan.

He slips in another one.

I say, "Hey, careful!"

When he tries for a third, I protest and clench my buttocks, and he stops, laughs, removes them.

I relax and suddenly he's back inside me. Amazingly now though, he feels much bigger – huge in fact. I try to move up onto all fours, try to touch myself but Ben resists, holding me down. "No, lie down," he orders.

His movements become more frantic, his breath against my back makes the hairs on my neck stand on end, and I am brought to a slow, aching orgasm.

I am amazed – for it's the first time I ever had an orgasm without involving my dick. I actually didn't know it was possible.

Ben judders to a groaning halt only seconds after, and collapses onto my back.

"Wow," I say.

Ben laughs. "Good?"

I nod; I roll sideways. He lies on the bed beside me. "Yeah, quite impressive," I say.

"Aha, it's not the ingredients, it's what you cook with them!" he laughs.

We lie side by side and smoke cigarettes. "I always do it that way," he says. "Actually I have trouble coming otherwise; sometimes it shocks people though..."

I drag on my cigarette. "What's to be shocked at? It was wonderful."

Ben smiles at me, runs a fingertip over my eyebrow. "Not everyone likes it," he says.

"What? Being fucked?" I ask. "I'm not always an aficionado myself."

He frowns at me. "You *did* realise didn't you?"

I raise my cigarette to my mouth, then pause. "Realise what?"

Ben snorts.

"What?" I ask.

He laughs again.

"What?" I insist.

"Nothing," he says. "Can you stay the night or?" I look at my watch, I had forgotten, it is three a.m.

"Shit. I have to get up in..." I count, "One, two, God! In three and a half hours!"

Ben watches me dress. "I'll call you when I get back," he says.

I nod noncommittally. I'm thoroughly convinced that he won't, and more importantly I am protecting myself from any emotional engagement. I don't want to ruin my holidays thinking about an illusory relationship back in France. *Been there, done that...*

I pull on my pullover, open the front door.

"Happy Easter," he says. He sniggers as he closes the door.

I frown as I walk away. *"Strange man,"* I think.

I slide between my sheets – they feel luxurious and crisp. My skin feels tingly and smooth. Sex often makes me feel that way, like a cat stretching in sunshine.

At six-thirty, I drag myself from my bed, sling the toothbrush and the razor into my pre-packed bag and stumble from the door into the cold morning air.

Easter Surprise

By eight-forty-five, I am halfway to Rome, the first stop. At eleven-thirty, I am somewhere over Israel wondering if the guy with the beard is going to explode the aeroplane over Tel Aviv. Qantas are serving Chicken Satay and simultaneously showing *Chicken Run*. A sort of Easter *thang* I guess, but I'm glad to be a vegetarian.

I squeeze past the guy with the beard, push down past the trolley, still serving drinks, beat the queue to the toilets.

Travel always does this to me. Air travel, time differences, microscopic toilets, all hope of regularity is lost. My guts feel strange and in the tiny room, wedged between the fold down baby tray and the dolls-house sink, the relief is wonderful and immediate.

I wipe, I stand, I reach for the flush lever. I freeze.

Lying in the pan is an egg. A perfectly ordinary, intact, peeled, hard-boiled egg.

"What the hell?" I think. It takes a while to realise where it has come from.

I pause, exhale and shake my head. I picture him laughing, saying, *"Happy Easter."*

"Bastard!" I say.

Members Only

An internationally renowned gay-fest, in the gayest and most beautiful city in the world, that's what the Qantas magazine says. I arrive in Sydney with little time to spare, shell shocked by the journey. I call in to Oxford Street where I guess I can buy tickets for the party. The street is abuzz with beautiful bronzed boys, muscle-bound men, and plain old-fashioned, screaming queens.

"This," I think, *"is a bit more like it! Statistically much more chance of meeting Mr right."* But how dreadful, to meet Mr Right on the other side of the world...

I stumble across the ticketing queue immediately and insert myself at the end of it. I am feeling woozy from jet lag and lack of sleep, but I am terrified that if I leave it until tomorrow, the day of the Mardi Gras, the tickets will be sold out. The queuing is good tempered, quiet conversation buzzing with expectation, foreign accents abound.

The sun is shining and I think, *"Maybe I could live here, if I did meet someone..."*

Finally after thirty-four hours travel and two hours queuing, I get to the counter. I have a brief panic attack – *Will they take my Visa card or should I have taken out some cash?* But I needn't worry about my credit card.

"Membership card?" The guy smiles at me hand outstretched. His accent is thick, pure Ozzy.

I frown at him. *"Membership* card?"

The smile disappears; the man rolls his eyes and repeats, seemingly for the fiftieth time today, "You can't buy tickets to the party unless you're a member of Mardi Gras."

I don't get it. The idea that the internationally renowned, international gay-fest is a member's only affair is more than my mind can grasp. "Member?" I repeat. "But that's insane, I live in *France."*

I start to feel annoyed. That tired, feverish kind of annoyed that happens when you travel for two days to a party but can't get in.

"You should have joined before you came." He shrugs bitchily.

"But I just queued for two hours!" I protest lamely. "Can I join now?"

"No, it takes a week. You should have done it over Internet mate," the guy replies. His voice goes up at the end of every sentence. Every line sounds like a question. Do I detect that he is enjoying this or is it just jet-lag paranoia?

"Maybe you should tell people in the queue about that." I am getting annoyed and I am feeling a little trembly. I know that I will have to leave before I explode. "So there's like, *no way?*" It is my last, unconvincing, feeble attempt.

"Unless you ask a mate who's a member, they can buy three tickets each."

I shake my head. "I live in France. I don't *have* any mates here."

The guy shrugs; I shamble outside.

I announce to the crowd, shouting, burning calories, emptying angst, that if they aren't members there is, "No bloody point queuing." A large group forms around me. Briefly I imagine us storming the ticket office but the group simply disperses groaning into Oxford Street.

I decide to convince someone, anyone, left in the queue, to buy an extra ticket for me. I shout to them all – no answer. I shout *at* them all.

I am proud of my bravery, but they all just stare at their feet.

I make my way back to the hotel on a lethally driven, diesel-pumping bus. It speeds along, way over the speed limit, with little or no regard for red lights or standing passengers. It reminds me of Italian public transport. Actually the driver *looks* Italian.

At the hotel I read the glossy Sydney guidebook, thoughtfully provided. It opens with the following phrase:

Sydney, the penal colony with an early case of perpetual anxiety about its chances of survival has turned out not to be an introspective, insiders city like its southern sister Melbourne, known to Sydneysiders as "Bleak City". As novelist Thomas Kenally said - Melbourne sometimes seems to be a secret to which you can obtain the code only if you are born into it or undergo a long initiation.

"*Or have a membership card?*" I think angrily.

I read on: *the word Melburnian, Kenally suggests, has a serious patrician resonance to it, whereas Sydneysider is a shack-dwelling beach combing sort of a word.*

"*How strange,*" I think, "*for a city to define itself primarily by what it is not.*"

And how strange, for Sydney to be primarily not Melbourne. Melbourne, which always struck me as such a funky, charming city, in a skinny-cap crystal-healing kind of a way.

I drift into a deep, jet-lagged, angst-filled slumber.

And You Thought You Were Gay?

The next morning, I awaken late and woozy. I pick up a second leaflet – this time a *gay* guide to Sydney – from the hotel desk and head off for coffee in a nearby café. This guide informs me that Sydney is, "the most beautiful city in the world." *"What about Venice, and Paris, and Prague?"* I wonder. They're all supposed to be OK-ish.

The guide also explains about Sydney's efficient network of buses, boats and trams. *No rat-infested sewer trains in this city sweetie*, it proudly proclaims.

I'm starting to feel a little anti-Sydney, but I decide to fight it. I know from experience that it won't help my holiday experience *at all*.

Unfortunately that evening the efficient buses aren't running to Taylor Square because of the Mardi-Gras parade, so I take a taxi and get stuck in traffic diverted around the carnival trajectory.

I watch the counter climb and wonder how much that makes in French Francs, or even more complicated how much in the soon-to-be-introduced Euros.

As I get out to walk it, I wish there *was* a rat-infested sewer train.

Taylor square is throbbing; people are excitedly reserving their viewing positions. A huge advertising hoarding dominates the square – it shows a woman with her tits popping out of the top of a Wonderbra. The caption reads: *And you thought you were gay.*

It strikes me as sexist, patronising and homophobic. I wonder what reaction would be to a poster showing a man's dick with the caption: *And you thought you were straight.*

Strange men are trying to sell me milk crates for anything from five to fifteen dollars. I reckon that they're impractical gifts and that I'll take back koala fridge magnets instead.

I go for a drink and chat to a couple of lesbians from Leeds in England. We drink too much. As the girls get louder they rope some cute Kiwis into our group.

Everyone is talking about Sydney. The girls agree with the Kiwis that Sydneysiders, *"have their heads up their arses."*

A sudden movement announces the beginning and we all rush outside. It has started and I finally understand the milk crate thing, but a little late.

We are faced with an impenetrable wall of backs, four people deep and three milk crates high.

We run up and down frantically, (a lot of people are doing this I notice), trying to peer through nooks and crannies, but I can see nothing.

After twenty minutes, I move over to a topless guy with Wonderbra pectorals. "Can I can stand on your crate for a few seconds," I ask, desperate to know what's happening on the other side.

"Nope," he says.

I turn to the guy next to him, who is looking down at me, smiling. He shakes his head. "Sorry."

"The locals are friendly," I say.

His smile fades. "What is your problem?" he asks.

I start to feel angry again. "My problem is flying for two fucking days to look at a row of backs," I shout.

He shrugs. "Yeah, well sweetie, some of us had to walk *minutes* to get here," he simpers. He turns back to watch whatever he's watching. I consider pushing him over and imagine the whole row falling like dominoes, but just in time, an American girl next to him jumps down. "Here! Use mine!" she offers, grinning.

Kylie Minogue is blaring from one of the floats. *Nah nah na, nah nah nah nah nah...*

I smile at her and climb up. Thirty or forty men in red sequinned shorts are dancing in formation, showing their waxed bodies. They are followed by forty drag queens running around in a headless-chicken figure-of-eight movement. Aware of hogging my host's milk crates, I jump down.

"So?" she asks.

It all seems a little empty to me – a little content-less, but I can't put it into words, so I shrug.

"I know," she says wrinkling her nose. "Once you've seen one butt in sequined shorts, you've seen them all."

I thank her and wander off to a bar and drink another beer. I can feel it all sloshing around in my stomach. I speak to a Scottish girl who says she's been living here a year. I'm feeling a little drunk again.

I say, "I *was* thinking of coming and living here. The gay scene is supposed to be so cool."

She laughs. "Aw for God's sake," she says, her accent thicker than ever. The words whistle out of her mouth. "Don't come here for that! They're *so* up themselves!"

I giggle.

"They're worse than the English," she adds.

When she leaves, her stool is taken by a guy: balding head, clipped hair, stubble, square chin, bold eyebrows. A sort of young Bruce Willis; he asks me where I'm from.

"How does it feel to be in the most beautiful city in the world?" he asks.

"People keep saying that," I say, "but who decides these things? Who decides that Sydney is better than Barcelona, or Rome?"

He gets up. "Winging pom," he says, as he moves away across the bar.

I get maudlin and push through the crowd to another bar.

A guy comes up and speaks to me. "Hi! You're cute," he says.

I grin. I start to breathe again.

He says, "Having fun?"

I try to look lit-up and enthusiastic. Then I let my features drop; I shrug. He looks so disappointed that I force the words out. I say, "Yeah, sure, it's great!"

He says, "There's a sauna next door. My boyfriend is waiting."

I smile uncomprehendingly. "You better get going then," I say.

He smiles and leans in until his face is almost touching mine. "I thought you might come too?" he says.

I smile. "Nah, you're alright thanks," I say.

He laughs. *"No?"* His voice is incredulous.

I grin at him; I shrug. "Sorry, yeah, I mean, yeah, the answer is *no.*"

He blows through his lips and shakes his head. "Crazy planet!" he says.

I bite my lip and frown. *"Crazy planet?"*

He shrugs, already turning away. "Yeah man," he says. "Like *you* refusing *me!*"

I feel homesick and utterly miserable, so I decide to go back to the hotel.

I stand in the midst of the international gay-fest waiting for a taxi. The crowd is diminishing and I imagine that they are all going to the party. I wonder how they got tickets.

The sign shouts at me. *And you thought you were gay.*

And I wonder. Sometimes I really do.

"Time to move on," I decide.

At the hotel I open my wonderful book: *Night Letters* by Robert Dessaix – a Melbourne man, please note.

I nod to myself as I start to read. "Tomorrow Melbourne!" I say quietly.

The Universe Lets Us Down

The night before it happens, we sit up till the early hours. We're talking out the big stuff in the garden and then, as the temperature drops, in the little purple lounge, sitting on the floor around bottles of beer. God, destiny and free will – it's years since I have discussed this stuff. It takes me back to my college years.

Owen's Australian wife gets bored with us and turns in at the beginning of the evening. She lives with the certainty that Buddhism is the only true religion. From that perspective she can't see what's to argue about, which seems fair enough. Faith, you've either got it or you haven't.

Owen moves with increasing difficulty to the fridge for more beers and in the alcoholic fog, lanes are explored and then abandoned simply because we forget which way we're going.

But in the morning when I awaken, I remember my problem.

I have been arguing that The Universe, The Force, or God for those who prefer, does not control what happens to me – I believe in free will.

And if God or the Infinite, or the System, is up there simply answering my own prayers, satisfying my own desires, creating the universe that *I* believe in, then why am I still single? Why am I so lonely? Why is my life so far from how I had hoped?

I have never really prayed, but this morning, as I wake up, I do. Not to any particular God – certainly not a mean judgemental man with a beard – but sticking to my theory of a benign force, I send out a call into the universe; I ask it for help.

I say, "I am sad and lonely. I need someone to share my life with. I need someone I can consider attractive, someone who makes me laugh, someone to build a history with. I'm sick of going on holiday on my own."

I send it into the universe and forget about it.

We rumble out of Melbourne to St Kilda on the tram, wander along the seafront, and then take seats in a café. The gentle summer sun bounces off the walkways. People loll around on every available inch of grass or beach while roller-blades energetically thrust past.

I watch a man jog along the promenade past us, and pause speaking momentarily, almost unnoticeably. For an instant his body has filled my mind.

He's tall, with dark short hair, rounded friendly features. He has a square jaw, jogger's thighs.

He trots by, and Owen and I continue talking, planning our journey south along the Great Ocean road. We order coffee.

The jogger speed-walks past in the other direction, and as he does so, as I turn my head to follow him, to fully appreciate this vision, he glances back. His brown eyes look puzzled, a half frown creases his forehead – I pause again but for longer.

Owen smiles at me knowingly. "What have you seen?" he asks.

"Oh nothing," I grin.

The coffees arrive. I drink and wipe the froth from my mouth.

The man walks past *again,* but this time looking at me with a nonchalant half smile on his lips. He heads off to the left towards the car park and my heart sinks. Giving up any attempt at conversation, I strain to watch him go.

And then, it happens and it is magical. He pauses, puts on his t-shirt and freezes, maybe thirty seconds in all, visibly deciding what to do. Then he turns back and starts walking towards us.

As he sits at the table next to ours, my heart starts to race; it feels terrible, the same way it felt when I met Robert, like a heart attack. I change seats to be able to see him better.

Owen asks if I'm OK – he's trying to talk to me, trying to tell me about a gallery in Canberra, but my mind is racing. Something tells me, something within me knows. This man is The One. He has been produced by The Force in response to my plea for help.

I try to think of a way to introduce myself, but my mind is a blank, everything seems cheap, stupid, obvious. It remains blank as he orders – his voice, smooth, rich, Canadian, I decide – and as he eats: oysters and salad, devoured with pleasure.

My heart's still racing. Between oysters he's glancing directly at me, his eyebrows raised into an amused question, a question not from him but from life: *"So this is what you wanted, will you now act?"*

I need to pull myself together.

I go to the bathroom to splash my face with cold water, but as I come out he's there, filling the doorway, smiling crookedly, waiting.

I try to speak. I actually open my mouth but nothing comes out.

"Like a tap in a derelict house," I think.

He nods at me, his mouth also open, his eyes huge and brown in the shadow of the interior.

I close my mouth; I smile.

He's nodding, encouraging me – but nothing comes, not a single sound.

We stare at each other in silence.

The tension is unbearable and at the same instant we are both overcome by it; he stands aside and I walk past.

Owen gives up trying to talk to me and frowns at me in concern.

Dejectedly I watch the man pay his bill, leave a tip, put on his baseball cap, and for the last time ever he walks past me.

He looks sad, as if life has let him down. He walks to the car park, and then, with a final glance backwards he disappears behind the wall.

And I think, *"The universe never lets us down. We do that all on our own."*

Any Friend Of The Egg Man...

I stare at my computer screen – the image is terrifying: an over-inflated version of Sylvester Stallone in Speedos. I stare at it, try to decipher my own feelings. In a strange, contradictory way I find it sexually thrilling but physically repulsive at the same time. I imagine the look on the guy's face when I take *my* kit off. *"No!"* I say to myself.

I click on reply: *... so really, if you're looking for another guy like you, well I'm afraid it isn't me...*

I sigh as I click on *send* – he sounded so nice in his first email, I had quite been looking forward to seeing his photo. Still, I tell myself, the ad will bring other replies.

My phone rings almost immediately. "Hi it's Alan," says a self-assured voice.

"Alan?" I say. "Sorry... I..." This doesn't sound like the Alan I know.

Alan laughs. "I sent you my photo, the body-builder..." His voice sounds polished and professional, like someone from TV, or a family doctor.

I frown. "Oh, look... Alan... How did you get my number?"

"It was at the bottom of your email," he says. "Sorry, maybe I shouldn't have called?"

"No, I'm sorry, it's fine," I say, already turning off the automatic signature in my email software. "I didn't realise I'd left... Anyway..."

"Look, I can call you back another time if you prefer."

"No it's fine, really."

"I just wanted to explain, about the body building thing."

I grin. "So that really *is* you?"

Alan laughs. "Yeah, I'm afraid so. It scares a lot of people off, which, as you can imagine wasn't the idea at all. I just wanted to speak to you so you'd realise that I'm not some kind of dumb beefcake."

"I never thought you were," I say. It's a lie of course.

We meet in a bar in Cannes.

The sun is setting over the blue Mediterranean; the light is warm and orangey.

Muscle man is already there when I arrive, only he's tiny – he never mentioned his height: a sort of pocket-sized action man. He's wearing a heavy sky-blue shirt; his physique is perceptible beneath it.

He looks tanned and healthy.

He grins when he recognises me and stands. He smiles broadly and shakes my hand – a firm, comfortable handshake, much like my doctor's.

I sit down and break into a grin.

"What?" he asks, his eyes flashing in amusement.

"What do you do for a living?"

He raises his eyebrows. "Now that's straight to the point."

I shake my head. "Sorry, it's not... I just have an idea. Since the second I heard your voice actually."

He smiles on one side of his mouth. "So, guess!" he says.

"Doctor?"

He laughs.

"That far off then?"

Alan shakes his head. "No exactly right, I'm a G.P."

I clap my hands together. "Huh!" I say. "I knew it."

"And you presumably work as a clairvoyant?" he laughs.

We talk about bodybuilding, sport, the gay scene, Internet. He's charming and intelligent and personable. We talk about holidays and camping and motorcycles. He smiles a lot and his eyes half close when he does – I like it.

The waiters are stacking chairs so we move next door to the pizzeria. We order food and a carafe of rosé.

We talk about religion and Alan tells me he was brought up as a Muslim. "But it seems to me, that anyone intelligent, well they're going to realise that any religion claiming to be The Only Truth is almost certainly going to be wrong, I mean, just with the number of religions and the law of probability," he says. He raises a finger to his lips. "I hope I'm not offending you," he says.

I shake my head. "Not at all," I say. "I mean, I believe in something, but I can't bear most religions. Being gay I can't really see how anyone can... It just doesn't strike me as compatible."

Alan gulps at his water. "Thank God!" he says.

We laugh and talk about racism, about his childhood in Morocco. He tells me about his ex boyfriend. He says he has never loved anyone that much before.

"I doubt I ever could again," he admits. "We're really close now though, it's as though we were never anything but friends. Weird, after nine years as a couple."

I say, "Wow! Nine years."

I tell him that I have a friend at work who is also a bodybuilder. "Maybe I should introduce you two," I say. "You never know." I wiggle an eyebrow.

Alan nods. "Oh," he says. "So I wouldn't... I mean... you wouldn't, personally...?" He shrugs.

I blush slightly. "Oh, I don't know, I mean..." *What do I mean?*

"You're nice, it's maybe a bit early for me to know," I say.

Alan smiles at me, places a hand on my arm. "Sorry," he says. "That was unnecessary. Of course."

"No, all I meant is that Xavier absolutes fantasises about going out with another muscle man. He'd *definitely* go for you."

"Personally," says Alan, "I find *you* quite attractive, but introduce me to your friend by all means."

This time I *really* blush; I can feel it. I hate that about myself, it always strikes me as such a feminine trait.

"You're blushing!" he says, pointing at me.

I love it even better when people point it out. *Like I didn't know.*

Our pizzas arrive and I am happy for the distraction. "Have you had many dates – by Internet I mean?" he asks.

I shrug. "Maybe five. I mean I've gone to meet about five of them. I got lots of replies, but they were mostly weirdoes."

Alan nods, forks pizza into his mouth.

"Actually some of the ones I *did* go and meet turned out to be pretty strange too."

Alan smiles at me. "Tell me. I need the warning. I've only just started."

I sip at my wine; I laugh. "Oh there are so many. I could tell you about the Egg Man! He was funny! But I'm not sure that you'd want to know. It's a bit far out. And a bit gross."

I realise that I didn't actually meet the Egg Man via Internet, but decide it's not important; it's a great story.

"The who? Is it an S&M story or something?"

I shake my head. "Might put you off your pizza though." I glance at his pizza. It has egg on it.

Alan laughs. "I'm a doctor. You can tell me!"

And so I tell him the story. "Imagine!" I say, "Sliding an egg into your partner's arse without asking! Jesus!"

"And you didn't like having an egg... You know?" He nods at me, wiggles his eyebrows. It's not the reaction I was expecting.

I frown. "Well, the actual experience of it was OK, because I didn't know. It made up for his *tiny* dick anyway." I raise a little finger to show him what I mean.

He nods at me. "So you *did* like it."

"Well it couldn't have worked anyway, I was leaving for Sydney the next day, he was moving to Paris, and anyway, anyone who does that has got to be a bit strange really, don't you think?"

Alan nods and gulps at his wine.

I lean in towards him. "He actually said he couldn't come otherwise," I tell him.

Alan shrugs.

I grit my teeth. *"Maybe Alan likes having an egg up his arse. Maybe it's his favourite sexual practice,"* I think.

"Of course, that wasn't the only problem," I say, trying to worm my way out. "He was a bit of a jerk in other ways too."

Alan puts down his fork and scratches his head.

"And he had like *no* sense of humour," I lie, shaking my head.

Alan carefully folds his napkin and places it on the table. He stands, very slowly, very rigidly.

I frown at him; he doesn't look well. He pulls a banknote from his pocket and places it on the table under the ashtray.

"I'm sorry," he says. "I have to go." His voice is rigid, icy.

My mouth falls open; I wrinkle my brow. "Did I say some..." I start to ask, but he has turned his back and is already walking away.

I stroke my beard. I stare at the sky for inspiration.

Alan walks twenty meters, and then pauses. When he turns to look back at me, I nod encouraging him to return.

He walks robotically back to the table, crouches beside me and stares into my eyes. *"Do doctors nut people?"* I wonder.

"Listen," he says.

I nod.

"Ben – that was his name?"

I open my eyes wide and bite my bottom lip. I grimace and nod.

"So the *Egg Man* does have a name."

I nod again; my teeth ache with embarrassment. His voice has started to lose its calm – started to rise in tempo and pitch and volume.

"Ben, or the *Egg Man* as you call him, is *the* most beautiful person I have ever met." His eyes are watering; his hand is shaking. "You have no right to insult him. What do you think you're doing? Going around telling people about that stuff! Don't you think he might *mind* in God's name?"

I nod childlike, grind my teeth.

His voice breaks, wobbles then finds itself and comes rushing out banging around the terrace. "Jesus! If you had the chance to have that wonderful man in your life, and you let him get away, then you are the most complete *jerk* that I have ever met!"

I stare at my plate and nod. "Sorry. I didn't..." I say. But he's gone.

I look at the banknote fluttering in the breeze and glare at the woman beside me. She's staring at me. *"What?"* I shout. She looks away.

I pull my own banknote from my wallet, slip it under the ashtray, and stand.

Bordeaux Biker

It's a long way to go for sex – that's the general opinion of most of my friends. And it's true that it will end up being expensive sex too: the hour-long plane journey alone is costing me over a thousand Francs.

But of course we aren't really talking about mere sexual fulfilment here. As W. H. Auden said, *All promiscuity is the search for an ideal friend*, and Louis could just be my ideal friend.

He's tall, brown and handsome, he surfs the Atlantic waves in the summer, and cycles along the coast in winter. He has a good job, makes me laugh, and looks devastating in his motorbike gear.

His face isn't very clear on the photo he sent, it's true – but he has an important job, and I understand that he doesn't want semi-pornographic photos (his motorcycle pants leave little to the imagination) circulating to all and sundry.

To punish him, I have sent an equally vague photo of myself, taken before I shaved off my beard.

His emails have been more and more enticing as the three weeks since we first chatted have gone by, and as I board the plane I'm trembling with excitement.

He has managed to make me laugh out loud telling me how his new secretary at work fancies him, and he has already given me an erection telling me about the wonderful open-air sex he had with his previous boyfriend during their camping holiday.

He's picking me up from the airport on his Suzuki (I have already imagined my legs clasped around his thighs) and we are heading off to his place in the country (yes this man has an apartment in Bordeaux as well as a house near the coast).

Saturday, we will walk along the sand dunes and eat in a little seafood restaurant he knows at the edge of the ocean. In the evening he's going to show me around Bordeaux's nightlife.

Sunday we're going on an all day outing with the local branch of the gay motorcycle club – so a long way for sex, but maybe not too far for a long weekend with an ideal friend. And if for some reason it doesn't work out, well, he has a spare bedroom.

As I come out through the barriers I see him. He's not tanned but this I can forgive, this is January after all. As I approach I see that he's beautiful, his blond hair has grown and is pulled back into a ponytail, it suits him wonderfully. As I walk toward him he sees someone beside me and runs past sweeping her up in his arms. This leaves me feeling confused.

Then I *really* see him – the man in motorbike leathers.

Louis is paler than in the photo – this I can forgive, this is January.

Louis is fatter than in the photo – at least twenty kilos heavier.

Louis is older than in the photo – late forties rather than mid thirties.

Louis is uglier than in the photo – no he's not ugli*er*, he's *ugly*. His skin is pitted and yellow tinged.

He walks towards me tentatively, he isn't sure about my identity and I am frozen.

"Mark?" he asks me holding out a hand. *"C'est toi?"*

I am panic-stricken. I have the seed of an idea, just an acorn of a plan, but it seems so mean... *Would I dare?*

He grins at me, his teeth are brown and uneven, his lips are pitted and rough.

Now we are face to face, I look him in the eye.

"Hi!" I say in my thickest American twang. "You must be Michelle's husband... She didn't tell me you were a motorcyclist! Hey I hope you're not intending to take me anywhere on a motorcycle! I've never been on one in my life!"

Louis frowns at me.

"I'm sorry," he says. His accent in English is thick.

"Is Michele with you?" I ask.

"I think you... Someone else." He waves a hand in the air as if this will help explain and shuffles past me.

I pretend to recognise someone further away. "No problem," I tell him generously.

He apologises again, and glancing back at me only once, turns ever hopefully to watch the stream of arrivals.

I wander off looking for the hotel desk. I feel shabby and dishonest.

"But he wasn't exactly honest either," I think, already justifying it to myself.

Love Me, Love My Life

We meet over the Internet – he answers my ad. We chat away via email, converted into electronic impulses, catapulted around cyberspace. It takes a while to build up a picture of him. We start with photos of ourselves, and end with photos of our families. We tell each other what we do for a living and end with our most traumatic life-events. Slowly I grow to like him, to look forward to talking to him on the phone.

Of course I don't really know him, so I suppose that this is the same loveliness present in every human being if we can only see it, but I come to know him as kind and fragile and I start to imagine his arms around me.

He lives in Paris. *"Still,"* I think, *"it's better than New York or Chicago!"*

But now, standing at the station, waiting for his train to roll in, I am terrified, for I've done this before and I know that tall can turn out to be short, thin to be fat, intelligent to be dumb. A dream can turn into a nightmare – I'm amazed that I still dare do Internet dates at all.

The train is late so I smoke a cigarette. "Mark!" – A voice to my right, a woman's voice.

I turn. I say, "Shit," under my breath. "Hi Carol!" It's Carol from work and I hate her. She thinks anyone with HIV should be put on an island somewhere, says that the Cubans have got it right.

"What are you doing here?"

I shrug. "Waiting for a friend," I say.

She nods. "I'm off to Marseilles for the weekend," she says, then, "A friend?" She cocks her head slightly as she says this.

I nod.

"Well I'd better be getting going," she says peering up at the notice board. "Oh no! My train is... Oh dear! Ten minutes!" she sighs. "Lucky I bumped into you then," she adds. *"Quelle chance!"*

I nod and say, "Yeah." – *"Ouais."*

"What train is your friend arriving on?"

"The TGV," I say. "From Paris."

"And how do you know each other?"

I peer at the notice board, buying time. "Our parents er, knew each other, um, when we were kids," I say.

She smiles and nods. "That's nice, so you've known each other for ever."

I nod. "Uhuh."

"But what if we don't recognise each other?" I think. "Shouldn't you be getting to the platform?" I ask.

Carol is pulling a packet of cigarettes from her jacket. "Nah, I'd rather stand here with you than stand alone on the platform!" she laughs.

The tannoy hollers that Luc's train has arrived. I roll my eyes and smile bravely at Carol.

I see him at a distance, pushing through the turnstile, his sports bag hiked up over his shoulder. He looks exactly as he did in the photo, I sigh with relief. He has recognised me and he's grinning from ear to ear.

"He looks happy to see you!" says Carol.

"Yes," I reply.

"Mark!" he exclaims. He drops his bag at my feet and hugs me heavily, awkwardly. He looks at Carol. "Hi," he says holding out a hand. "Luc."

Carol gives a little nod, holds out her hand. "Oh well, I better go and catch my train," she says picking up her bag.

"So!" breathes Luc, as Carol starts to walk away. "We finally get to meet face to face!"

I close my eyes in pain and when I open them Carol has paused – she's looking back with a crooked smile spread across her lips. She's staring at me. "Well have a good weekend with your *old old* friend," she says.

I smile tightly at her.

"You can tell me all about it on Monday," she says pushing off through the turnstile.

Luc looks at me questioningly. "Are you OK?" he asks. His voice is lovely, his hug is huge and warm, and I think this may just turn out OK.

As we drive out of the city, as the dual carriageway becomes single carriageway and single lanes become country lanes, as the sun sets to our left, the conversation is warm and polite.

We're edging around each other, lifting little inspection hatches, peering in, excitedly exploring with an eye for major structural faults, but none appear yet. He tells me he was listening to Monty Python on his Walkman, that his laughter made the woman opposite so uncomfortable that she changed seats.

We laugh and slowly relax.

At the house he tries to hug me again, and he kisses me.

We have to try, we have to see how it feels, what will happen. But all we learn is that it's too soon, that we are too rigid, that we are still too separate for a kiss to prosper, so we abandon and occupy ourselves with dinner.

Luc watches me cook. He can't cook anything himself, he says.

We drink glasses of Bordeaux and chat as I chop vegetables and beat eggs.

As the rain starts, then lashes against the kitchen window; as the omelette bubbles and pops before me, we enter the comfort zone.

No longer hunting for the next subject, the conversation flows easily, the kitchen feels warm and nocturnal and cosy. He steps into my space, stands before me.

He says, "I'm really happy to be here with you after all this time."

I grin; we kiss. I sigh. I'm happy too.

For dinner we sit at the big wooden table. He loves my table, he says. In Paris he eats in the kitchen, on Formica.

I picture the frozen microwave meal and I feel sad for him.

We talk until the early hours and drink too much, smoke too much, tell too much. We have typed everything before, but saying it is different. The route from vocal cord to eardrum is incomparable to words converted into bits and bytes – electronic impulses and radio waves or light impulses – only to be converted all the way back again. No, this is different and I have a feeling we are going too far, that he's revealing too much too soon.

He says most of his friends have left Paris now; says he has been thinking of leaving, moving somewhere else, starting afresh.

I yawn, mainly to close the conversation.

Immediately a problem arises: the sleeping arrangements. Of course we both hope to sleep together, hope to have wild lavish sex – it's the unspoken agenda for the meeting. But how to get there? How to move from this warm friendly *politesse*, to heaving bodies? How to do it without risk of offence?

When I offer him the spare room, he accepts.

I go to prepare the bed and he laughs and says, "If it's too difficult then I can always sleep somewhere else..."

I know where this is leading and I smile, I play the game. "There isn't really anywhere else," I say shrugging. "Unless you're intending to sleep in my bed."

He looks into my eyes. "It's a double," he says.

I start to laugh and put the sheets back in the cupboard.

We head to the bedroom. We kiss and cuddle; he's huge and warm. But he doesn't get an erection. "I'm sorry," he says. "It's not you. It happens all the time."

Maybe I should just forget it, let it drop, but that always sounds worse to me, less accepting, so I try to be routine about it. I try to chat about it, ask him how often, since when.

In the dark, his body starts to shudder, tears flow. I hold him until it stops and then until he drifts into sleep.

When I awaken in the morning our bodies are entwined. We roll around and giggle and laugh. I discreetly slide a hand over his limp cock and hiding my disappointment jump from the bed to make coffee.

The day drifts by easily, dreamily. We talk about our childhoods, our families. We prepare food and fill and empty the dishwasher.

Luc loves my dishwasher, he wishes he had one, but there's no room in his tiny flat.

We wander into town and drink coffee; Luc picks up the receipt. "Wow, half the price of coffee in Paris!" he says.

Some friends wander past and join us. They chat to us, calm and relaxed. They are very nice to Luc; they don't ask how we met. They lived in Paris before and we all agree to hate the city and love the trees and the lanes.

The sun is shining today, and I think how easy it is to love the countryside in the sunshine, and how I crave the city when it rains.

On the way back to the house Luc says that I am very lucky to have such lovely friends, very fortunate to have such a great life-style.

"Nothing is luck," I say. "Everything is choice." Luc doesn't agree.

In the evening I cook fish parcels, we open another bottle of wine.

He says he has to get away from Paris, has to break the *metro-boulot-dodo*, metro-job-sleep cycle he has suffered for the last nine years.

I say that many would consider him lucky to live there, to have museums and bars and restaurants and nightclubs.

Luc says that he never goes out anymore, that after a while one just doesn't bother. "I'd rather go and collect eggs from the chicken shed like you do," he says.

I feel anxious, a slight tightness across my chest, around my heart – I wonder why. The physical symptom always seems to be apparent long before the reason.

I ask him what music he wants to hear, but he doesn't have a preference, he likes all music. "It's so nice to have any music at all," he says. "My hifi has been broken for months."

I ask him how he spends his weekends. He says, "Oh normal stuff, you know, shopping, cleaning, watching TV. I'm usually really tired by the weekend. City life is very stressful."

"You don't seem to be very happy with your life," I point out.

His eyes darken; he shrugs. "It's true I suppose," he says. He laughs nervously. "Maybe I should just quit everything and come and live in Grasse! I feel happier here than I have for ages."

A cold front moves over my heart; I shiver. I light a log fire.

Luc says he loves log fires and as we sit before it, he grasps my hand. "I love this," he says. "I love being here, your house, the garden, the cat," he laughs. "I think I love you too."

It's too soon and it's all too much. And it's all the wrong way around. I can feel my heart closing down; feel the protection barriers going up, sense the drawbridge lifting. I don't *want* to be the all-in-one solution to anyone's problems. I wonder, *"Is that selfish?"*

Now it is my turn to feel sad – sad for Luc and his miserable life, and sad for the dream I will shatter at the end of the weekend.

And sad, above all, for my own enduring loneliness.

Luc picks up on my mood. He says, "It's OK."

But it isn't OK. It isn't OK at all.

Straight Night Out

I push open the door. Hot, smoky air blasts past us into the December night. Isabelle squeezes past me into the bar, already removing her woollen hat, unzipping her coat. The pub is busy, frenetic with alcoholic loudness, the English pretending to be in England, the French enjoying a cheap trip to British pub culture. I let the door slam behind me and follow her into the noise and smoke.

"You're right," she shouts over her shoulder. "The atmosphere's completely different!"

"Half of Antibes is English," I tell her.

We elbow through to the bar and I order pints of Guinness and cheese and onion crisps. Isabelle rips the bag open, tastes one and makes a face.

"All part of the experience," I tell her. I lift the drinks, turn to face her.

"So this place is straight is it?" she asks.

I nod.

She grins. "Good," she says.

"Why? Seen something nice?"

She nods. "Behind me, against the wall, black trousers, white shirt, green tie, balding, cute."

I lean to the left, peer over her shoulder. Isabelle turns, looks behind her.

The man looks at her then switches his regard to me. I grin as recognition slowly registers on his face.

Isabelle turns back to look at me, opens her hands. "So?" she says.

"Mark!" booms the voice behind her. "Bonsoir!"

I step past Isabelle, lean in to kiss him on the cheek but he holds out a stiff hand, blocks my path with it – I shake it.

He shoots a warning glance behind him. "Clients," he says simply.

I nod.

"Isa, meet Robert." They kiss.

Isa frowns, cocks her head on one side. "The Robert you told me about?"

I glare at her. "No!" I say.

Robert grins. "It's all lies!" he says. "Whatever it was."

Isa shrugs. "So you're not cute at all then?" she says with a laugh.

Robert points vaguely over his shoulder. "Look, I have to..."

I nod. "Sure."

"Can I call you though?"

I sigh. "Sure, I mean..."

"It has been ages Mark, I haven't seen Yves for *years,*" he says.

I smile. "I haven't seen him for a while either," I say.

A fat man in a three-piece suit appears at Robert's elbow. "More drink required," he says.

Robert nods and moves away towards a space at the bar.

"That's him right?" asks Isabelle.

"Yves' ex, yes," I say.

"The one who tried it on with you?" she asks.

I nod. I roll my eyes and grin.

"And you refused?" she asks incredulously, wrinkling her nose and glancing back at him.

I shrug. "He was with Yves!" I say.

She shakes her head. "You are *such* an arsehole!"

Big Shiny Jeep

I dream of a ship – of an alarm on a ship, of a ringing bell, of a screaming siren, images straight from *Titanic* which I saw last week. I drag myself from the depths of the sea and gasp for air. The siren still screams, no, not a siren, an alarm clock, no, a telephone...

I fumble for it to my left. I try to say, "Allo." Actually I say, "Ahhharh..." My mouth is too sticky.

The voice is buzzing, electric, and shockingly awake. "It's Robert. Did I wake you?"

I peer blearily at the red numbers on the alarm clock. "It's seven," I say vaguely. "It's Saturday."

He laughs at the other end of the line. "Sorry," he says. "I've been thinking about you. Since last night."

I don't tell him that I also thought about him, just before I went to sleep. I say, "Uhuh."

"Look, I'm going skiing today. Do you want to come?"

I cough to clear my throat and lift myself up onto one arm. "I... erh. I'm not sure," I say.

Robert laughs. "I know you're not," he says. "But I'm not asking you to climb Everest – just come skiing. I hate skiing on my own. You *do* ski don't you?"

I sigh. "Sure," I say. I wonder vaguely where I put my skis.

"Oh come on!" he insists.

I frown and roll my tongue around my sticky mouth. "What time are you leaving?" I ask.

It is a question. Robert takes it as an answer. "Great!" he gushes. "I'll pick you up at eight."

I cough. *"Eight?"*

"OK, eight-thirty."

I sigh. "You don't know where I live," I say. "I live in Grasse now."

He laughs maniacally, serial killer style. "I know more about you than you can possibly imagine," he says.

I hang up the phone, stare at it and shake my head. "Yeah well, you don't know what time I get up on Saturdays," I mutter.

His Jeep is Big and New and Shiny. I am relieved that I didn't volunteer my car. As I sit next to him, looking at his trendy military-style ski pants, his bulging arm filling his t-shirt sleeve, his chrome Breitling watch – as I sit nursing a slight hangover, a lack of sleep, and trying to close the stuck zip on my faded ski suit, I wonder if Robert isn't altogether *too* shiny.

He talks constantly. This is good – it enables me to doze.

"I prefer the north side," he's saying. "There are some great black runs, and in the early morning they're in full sunshine."

I roll my head towards him. "I don't do black runs," I say.

He laughs. "Except today!" he says.

I laugh back. "Not even today," I say.

Robert tells me at some length how the only way to advance in life is to face up to one's fears. I sigh. He's making me feel like a kid; making me want to tell him to shut up.

I let him finish and smile. "And the best way to break a leg is to ignore the fear," I say.

"You won't break a leg," says Robert.

I nod exaggeratedly, eyes wide. "I know. Because I won't be going down *anything* more difficult than a blue!"

The twists and turns of the road, my hangover and the tough suspension of the Jeep have contrived to push me to the edge of carsickness. On arrival I need coffee.

"You can have coffee later," says Robert. "We're going to make the most of all those empty slopes first." He clips into his skis and cuts and grooves down to the ski lift.

I wobble and slither after him. "I haven't found my feet yet," I offer apologetically.

He grins at me.

At the top we argue about which *piste* to take. I favour the blue, Robert the red. We compromise, go separate ways.

I arrive at the bottom feeling wobbly and uncoordinated. Robert who has been waiting for ten minutes is ready to move on. "Come on!" he says slewing away. "I'll show you the other side of the mountain!"

I sigh and push off after him.

We take a chair lift and the sun starts to gain power – my face glows with the cold air and the sunshine.

Robert drapes an arm around my back. "I thought you were a better skier," he says.

"I never really learnt. I mean I've never had any proper lessons." I light a cigarette.

He pulls away. "Sorry, but I can't bear cigarette smoke in the mornings," he says.

I blow the smoke the other way. It inevitably drifts back over him.

"I mean what is the point?" he continues. "Coming all the way up here to breathe in smoke?"

I toss my cigarette into the distance. For an instant, I flinch, waiting to be told off for this.

He smiles at me. "Thanks," he says.

At the top I get my coffee. Robert takes his back because it's cold.

Mine's actually cold too, but for some reason – due to some strange British quirk that I've never quite understood – I say, "No, mine's fine."

"OK. You did your blue. Now we do my black!" says Robert.

I prod him in the arm. I say, "Look into my eyes." I say, "It *isn't* going to happen. So find a new goal in life."

He laughs. "I love your British sense of humour," he says.

Robert points me off towards my gentle slither; heads off for his death-defying drop.

I slither away; I relax.

I watch clouds forming in the distance at the top of a mountain. I feel the air brushing the back of my neck; I see a flash of red as a nine year old hurtles past me.

"A full two kilometres of steady, smooth, descent! Now this is skiing!" I think, enjoying the sudden freedom of not having someone waiting for me at each bend.

As I round the first bend, my mouth drops. I panic and try to stop – I fall over, skid to the edge and look down at the drop. I look back up the slope at my lost ski pole.

A man in ski-school uniform stops beside me. "Where's the *piste?*" I ask him. He points to the drop.

"I can't go down *there!*" I say.

He shrugs. "You shouldn't be on a black slope then," he says, launching himself into the void.

I watch him zigzag around the bumps, descending directly beneath me.

I look back at the slope behind me and start to edge up to my ski pole. *"The bastard!"* I say.

It takes me two hours to get back to the station. Two hours of standing up, wobbling, slithering, gathering speed, falling. Two hours of brushing snow from my arse, of emptying snow from my gloves, of trying to warm my hands and of swearing at Robert.

When I arrive at the station I see him waiting, looking the other way.

I arc to the left, ski behind him and straight into a restaurant. I switch off my mobile phone and lie back on a cushioned bed-chair. I think about him trying to find me all afternoon – it makes me grin.

By five p.m. as the sun disappears from the last corner of my bed-chair, as the iced air suddenly starts to assert itself, I have calmed down.

118

I switch my phone back on; it rings almost immediately. "Oh thank God!" I say, "I was looking for you over on the other side. My phone didn't seem to pick up over there. Sorry."

"Have a good time?" he asks.

I can tell from the contrite tone of his voice that he knew exactly where he was sending me.

I say enthusiastically, "Fabulous actually."

We drive down in tired silence. We unload my skis outside my house.

I say, "I'm really busy tomorrow," and "I've got a really heavy week at work." He seemingly accepts this as the truth.

Control Freak

I open my eyes. The banging from my neighbours is deafening. I glance at the alarm clock. 9:02 a.m. I frown. *"Nine a.m. Sunday morning is not the time to put up more shelves,"* I think.

The banging continues. It's very loud. I stare blearily at the light filtering through the shutters. A voice says, "Come on! Wake up! It's a lovely day out here!"

I groan and swing my legs to the side of the bed. They ache from yesterday's falls.

The banging continues in little, short, staccato bursts.

I push my weight unsteadily onto my legs, pull a towel from the back of the sofa and wrap it around my waist.

I wander through to the kitchen, tripping on the end of the towel. "Yeah, yeah," I shout, reaching for the bolt and pulling open the heavy door.

Robert grins at me. "He lives!" he shouts theatrically. The loudness of his voice makes me half close my eyes.

He pushes past me. I stare wistfully at the empty space on the doormat where he had stood, and slowly turn back into the house, pushing the door closed behind me.

"You are sleeping your life away!" says Robert. My mother always used to say the same thing.

"Sleep is an essential part of life," I say. "Without sleep we *die.*" It's the defence my father used.

Robert is unpacking shopping on the kitchen table: oranges, bananas, high protein milk. "Sorry?" he asks. His voice indicates that he's not particularly interested.

"You have to sleep, that's all. Look what are you *doing* here?"

Robert looks up at me and shrugs. "Fixing you breakfast, what does it look like?"

I yawn; I sigh.

"Can we get some light in here?" he asks. "I take it the shutters do actually open?"

I nod. I wander to the window and push them open. They *clack* back against the wall. The sky is deep Mediterranean blue; the air is cold. Light rushes into the kitchen.

"Not a lot of point though," says Robert.

I look at him questioningly.

"Staying alive, if you're just going to sleep all the time."

I sigh heavily.

He lines up the six oranges on the table and glances at me. "So when you say that you're busy, that would be busy, like, *sleeping?*" he asks.

I nod. "Well I try," I say rubbing sleep from the corner of my eye.

"Very sexy," he says.

I force a grin at him. "Yeah well I haven't done my face yet," I say. "I wasn't expecting company."

Robert nods. "Nice towel too," he says.

I look down at my towel. It's yellow; it's a towel. I frown at him. "Call next time. I'll put on a suit," I say.

As he whisks past me towards the sink, he touches my chin. "I'd love to see you in a suit. I bet you'd look great. Huh! Imagine!" he laughs.

I sit at the table. I push a space between the books and magazines and Robert's breakfast articles for my elbows. I don't tell him that I wear a suit every day from Monday to Friday, that I have ten of them in the wardrobe. I just watch him in silence, one eyebrow raised.

"Well, *I've* already been to the gym *and* I've done my weekly shopping at the market," he says.

"Umh," I say. "Martha Stewart *would* be proud."

"Who?"

"Never mind. What are you doing?" I ask him. He's opening and closing the doors to all of my cupboards. It makes exactly the same noise as when he knocked on the door.

"Is there actually *any* logic to your cupboards?" he asks, slamming another door.

I half smile at him. "Not really. What are you looking for?"

"The juicer," he says.

I frown.

"Orange squeezer," he says.

"There isn't one."

He turns towards me and places one hand on his hip. "This is a man who doesn't have an orange squeezer," he says.

I open my eyes as wide as I can. I nod. "This is," I say.

Robert sighs. "You can tell so much about people from their cupboards," he says. "Yours are a disorganised mess. Jees, I can't even find any plates!" He lifts up a roll of scotch tape. "I mean, what's this doing here?" he asks.

I shrug.

"And the plates?" he asks.

I shake my head. "Sorry. All in the dishwasher."

Robert bends down, opens the dishwasher.

"It's dirty," I say.

"Then why don't you switch it *on?*" he asks.

The rapid-fire rhythm of his voice is winding me up. I imitate it. "Because it's *not full!*" I say.

Robert leans against the counter. "But you don't have any clean plates!" he says.

I feel slightly feverish, slightly dizzy. I realise I'm getting angry and sigh. "I didn't *need* any plates," I say, "I was *sleeping.*"

Robert smiles at me. "So cute, yet so dumb!" he says. "So, tell me, dearest Mark. You eat breakfast off the floor do you?"

I roll my lips into an 'o'. I stare at him. The patronising use of my name really bugs me; I chew the inside of my mouth. "When I *do* get up, well, I don't really *do* breakfast Robert," I say.

"You *don't?*"

I shrug. "Actually, most mornings I just eat a yoghourt."

Robert nods at me as though this is the strangest information he ever heard. "Yoghourt," he repeats.

I smile; I nod. "Yoghourt," I say.

He says, "Yoghourt," once again and turns to the refrigerator.

I roll my eyes at his back. "Robert look," I say. I raise a hand to my forehead.

He bends down, peers into the fridge.

"No-one asked you to come here," I say.

He pulls the bin to his side. He picks up an aubergine and drops it into the bin. "How can you live like this?" he asks.

"Robert, for God's sake!"

He drops some onions into the bin.

"They're fine, stop it!" I stand. "Will you just mellow out for Christ's sake?"

I walk over to him. "Get out of my fridge!" I say pushing him aside. I reach in, pull the yoghurt pack from the fridge and stuff it into his hands. I point to the dining table. "Sit!"

He sits with the yoghurts in front of him. He stares at them.

I sit opposite in silence. "What?" I ask eventually.

"Jesus!" he says.

I shrug. *"What?"* I wipe little beads of sweat from the side of my forehead.

"They're still in the cardboard," he says.

I nod. I scrunch up my eyebrows. "They *come* that way," I say.

He shrugs. *"Whatever,"* he says.

I shake my head. "No hang on," I say. "I don't get it... What's the problem with the cardboard?"

"Well you're *supposed* to unpack them *before* you put them in the fridge."

I shrug. "Who says?"

"Well it's like just dumping your shopping still in the carrier bag straight in the fridge."

I shrug again. "Sometimes I do that too. If I'm in a hurry."

Robert looks at me and slowly shakes his head.

"I couldn't be bothered, I was in a rush. That's all. So what?"

Robert nods knowingly. "Hum," he says.

"What?" I say.

He shrugs. "Your house is a mess." He gestures around him. "Your fridge is... disgusting." He nods at me. "But this, Mark." He taps the pack of yoghourts with a finger. "This is about as lazy as it gets."

I suck air through my teeth. I stand and walk over to him.

I pick up the oranges, the bananas, the Sports-Plus High-Protein Milk™. I put it all back in the bag. Robert looks up at me, he looks sad.

I grab his arm, lift him to his feet and lead him gently to the door, he doesn't resist. When I push the bag into his chest, his arms move up to hold it.

His eyes are deep dark pits; something tells me that this has happened to him before. A lot.

I shake my head and open the door, and silently he walks out.

As he opens his car door he glances back at me – he looks about twelve years old.

Country Life

It's February, nearly the end of another winter in this damned house. I've been looking at the small ads, toying with the idea of giving away the chickens and moving back somewhere where people just *drop-in* for coffee.

It seems that it hasn't stopped raining once since last September, only an impression, I know. I spend my time driving into Nice, invited to friends dinner parties, or going out for a drink, on my own, always searching, always hoping.

I'm battling through this with a forced smile on my face because I only have to think of my mother to know just how fast a social life can dwindle if you walk around with a face like a smacked arse. But the truth is, I hate it, I was never designed to spend evenings alone, staring at the rain, poking the coal fire, eating pasta in front of the TV.

I don't function properly alone, and though it's unbearable being in the wrong relationship, tonight it seems to me that nothing could be worse, truly *nothing* could be worse than this dreadful, droning emptiness.

I'm drinking too much: the pile of empty bottles to be recycled is proof enough. I am sinking into depression, which is of course why the mountain of empty bottles is still sitting there. I've called Claire twice this week; my drunken tears will end up terrifying her. Tonight I spare her.

Tomorrow I have a dinner with the gay motorcycle club, and tonight, as I go wearily to bed, that rare desire comes over me, the desire to pray. This only really happens in moments of desperation because I don't really believe in God, or certainly not God as we were taught at school, but I guess I believe in some vague kind of benign force. I don't tend to say it too loudly though; it sounds a bit Star-Warsy after all.

Lately, in this winter, this depression, this loneliness, I have been having trouble believing in anything at all. Even my friendships seem to have become complicated now that I am alone. People who have invited me to dinner for years, simply because they wanted to see me, now sound as though they are inviting me because they feel sorry for me.

When I ask them to dinner and they refuse, I am left wondering if I have not become so depressing that no one can bear my company. Maybe it's just paranoia, then again, maybe it's true – maybe I have become my mother. Maybe it *is* genetic after all and I will end up alone and on Prozac. Hell I *am* alone, and the only reason I'm *not* on the Prozac that the doctor gave me is that I'm too stubborn to take it.

So perhaps it's because I have reached the bottom of my pit, that I have ground my face down in this misery until I just can't bear it any more, or maybe it's something to do with Paolo Coelho's metaphysical story I read this morning, but whatever the reason, as I lie down, after I turn out the lights, just before I settle into a surprisingly restful slumber, I pray.

"Please help me. Please send someone to save me. I hate this. I don't deserve this. I can't stand it much longer." My breath shudders with the angst I am feeling, the edge of a sob. As I drift off, strangely, I have a feeling that I have been heard; I imagine the wheels of the universe already grinding, squeaky and slow, into a new, better configuration.

The next day the winter sun is out; the sky is a deep shade of blue. I feel refreshed and optimistic. I ride my motorbike to Antibes to charge up the battery. The motorbike too has been abandoned these last few weeks.

I sit in a café and for a while I enjoy it all: the bike, the cool air, the sunshine. And then I think of the wheels of the universe and I start trying to give it a helping hand.

I wander around town drinking coffee after coffee, hyping out on caffeine and watching every man who passes by. I wouldn't want to miss the one that the universe has sent, but of course there is no one and I start to feel sad, so I return home. I am fighting to keep my edge, fighting not to sink into another pit.

By eight p.m. when I have to leave, the outside temperature has plummeted to five degrees, so I take the car. As I drive I remember the prayer and add to it.

"Look, if you need an opportunity then here it is," I say. "If I need to act for this to happen then I'm acting. There will be fifty people there tonight and I only need one. I'm not asking for Tom Cruise, or Albert Einstein. Someone nice, someone I don't find physically revolting, someone who makes me laugh, someone I can be friends with, have fun with, talk to late at night as I drift off to sleep." As I say this I imagine a man. He has brown hair, a warm smiling face and he's winking at me. "If you can send him tonight," I add desperately, "then that would be perfect."

This strikes me as a little presumptuous. I wonder momentarily if it is possible to ask too much of an infinite force, it being infinite and all. Just in case I add, "Oh and if for some reason that's not possible, just a nice evening will do."

I know I don't mean it. I expect that The Force realises too.

I park the car and walk around to the front of the restaurant.

Two friends from the club are stamping their feet against the cold, talking into their mobile phones. I push inside and the noise and smoke and heat of the restaurant are momentarily overpowering. I force through the gathering towards the coat-stand, creaking, overloaded with heavy motorcycle gear.

As I wriggle out of my jacket and reach to hang it on the top of the pile, he's suddenly there, grinning at me. He says, "So where's the crash helmet?"

I feign embarrassment, bite my lip. "Sorry... Car," I say.

"Shame on you." He holds out a hand. "Hugo."

I freeze; I stare. I know that this is him. Even as I think it, it strikes me as ridiculous, but it feels like truth. It feels like someone somewhere in the universe has heard me, I grin stupidly and shake his hand.

He smiles at me, and he winks. He actually winks.

When the time comes to eat, I manoeuvre myself, or more precisely we manoeuvre ourselves, side by side. Hugo contributes by giving up his seat to fetch his wallet from his jacket. When he returns, the seats between us have been taken; he sits down next to me.

The meal is terrible but then they always are. "This is a motorcycle club not a gastronomic one," I say to someone who starts to complain. I don't care though, I am happy.

Hugo is a dancer and he's very funny. A touch of camp, a little finesse in every gesture, but also a biker, a drinker and a smoker, a great buzzing contradiction of humour, blokeiness, and elegance.

Someone is talking about organising a party – he needs go-go boys. "Hey what about Hugo?" asks Jean-Paul. "He is a dancer after all."

I grimace with embarrassment. Hugo tries to explain that contemporary dance isn't quite the same thing as gogo dancing.

I smile, warmed by his efforts to explain this without making his aggressor feel stupid. I feel as though I am sitting next to a log fire, as though I am warming my cold, frosty body next to it. I realise that I have been on the edge of hypothermia. Hugo is saved when five of us decide to join in, to jokingly conspire to harass him.

"Well it *is* dance, and it *is* contemporary," we say, "after all."

Jean-Paul cottons on, exaggerates along with the rest of us to demonstrate that, in fact, he was actually joking as well – that he intentionally initiated the joke and Hugo gives in, stands on his chair and shows us just how well he *could* do the job.

It's nothing; it's a mere joke. But we're all impressed by the roll and the groove of his body. Personally I am awe-struck.

"Hey, do you strip as well?" asks Jean-Paul.

Hugo slides back into his chair with a laugh. "Sure!" he says. "I'll strip. But I never go further than my flowery boxer shorts."

126

We laugh.

"Oh, and flip flops," he says. "I *never* dance without flip flops!"

We laugh, we drink, we fool around, and once or twice he mockingly pinches me.

As I drift off to sleep, I think of him, see his face, see the movement of his body, imagine stroking the smile lines around his eyes.

I know that I'm in love again and the world is transformed from a terrifying desolate winter into a playground of possibility, of snuggling in front of coal fires, and walking side by side through the frost. I think how hard the fall will be if this doesn't happen.

I try to stop hoping, try instead to work through all the reasons why it might not happen in my mind. But as I lie awake, revelling in the mere thought of him, as I hear the rain start again, I think it sounds beautiful.

The next day I call the club secretary. He gives me Hugo's surname: Damiano.

Monday is shopping day, it takes all day to find exactly what I am looking for. The name rolls around my head. "Hugo Damiano."

In the evening I look him up in the phone book, pack up the gift and seal the brown, padded envelope. I scrawl the address across the front. I remember, too late again, that it's easier to write while the envelope is still empty.

Tomorrow I will post them, and he will, or will not understand – it's a test. A test that this is truly the man the universe has sent, that he has noticed me, that he knows only I could have sent that package.

It's a test that he has the sense of humour to find it funny and more than anything that he can fall in love with someone who sends him flowery boxer shorts and flip-flops through the post.

I will not call though. He has the gift, and if the test fails then it must fail.

A week drags by. I cave in and call.

A man answers. "He's in Sweden. Working. Sorry," he says. "He'll be back on Friday though."

Funny that. I had thought of lots of reasons it might not work. But I never even imagined that he might not be single. *"How dumb. How stupid. How typical,"* I tell myself.

"It's his brother," says Isabelle when I call her. "Or a friend, or someone he lent his apartment to."

I hope, but I don't really believe. The week passes slowly. Finally Friday arrives. It grinds past like a bad film in slow-motion.

Saturday is worse.

Sunday, I start to feel like I'm getting over it. *"If he can't even be bothered to reply,"* I tell myself, *"then he's not worth worrying about."*

But I feel sad. I feel surprised and disappointed – I hadn't imagined this ending at all.

Monday evening arrives and I've pushed it from my mind. I put some pasta on to cook. Enough for one, again.

The cat sits on my lap in front of the fire, wide-eyed at the spitting wood.

The phone rings, I look at the number on the display; I stare at it, a *local* number. I wait till the last ring, the final ring before it goes onto voicemail then swipe it from the cradle.

"Hi it's Hugo," he says. "Do you remember me?"

"Hi," I say, "I erh..."

"I just wondered if you wanted to come to dinner, tonight, with some friends?" he says. "It's a bit late I know."

I shower, I shave, I tidy the bed.

I tip the pasta into the bin and push it down to hide it behind the rest.

The friends are actually half of the dance company. They are clever, pretty, and wild. They drink a lot, smoke a lot, laugh loudly and put me at ease.

The menu contains one hundred percent meat dishes, so I eat lettuce and raw carrots. Hugo says I'm, *"Qu'un villain lapin."* – Nothing but a naughty rabbit.

I manage to be funny, witty, and irreverent, I reflect my surroundings. I had forgotten just how "up" I can be. Red, smiling faces beam at me from around the table.

Everyone says goodnight, including Hugo. The company are invited somewhere for drinks; they are leaving me behind.

I stand nonplussed, next to my car, watching them climb into theirs, and then, just as Hugo lifts a leg to get into the last car, he changes his mind. He runs across the car park and kisses me, deep and hard. I am so surprised that I don't move.

He grins. "I'll call you tomorrow," he says.

And thus it starts. We sleep in his house; we sleep in my house. We build towering inferno log-fires and roll around in front of them.

We drink too much, argue about everything, agree in the end, and have sex again. He loves my mess; I love his heaps of junk. It feels relaxed and easy and right.

"I had forgotten how easy it could be," I tell Isabelle.

We hang out with his friends from the company. I feel like a student again, feel the way I did before, when I was young, when all that mattered was having a laugh. I feel the way I felt before I started shopping at *Habitat*.

I realise that my life has been so empty. That living in the middle of nowhere, being made redundant, and being single, huh! No wonder I was feeling depressed, Hugo is my very own universal solution.

He fills my mornings, my lunchtimes, my evenings and my nights. He's so hyperactive that I need the time when he's working just to catch up on my sleep quota.

We spend half of our time alone, the other half with his friends, his colleagues, his family. When he goes away, sometimes I get to travel with him: we go all over France, to Amsterdam, to Prague, to Seville. When he gets complimentary tickets to some cultural event he takes me with him, and he gets *a lot* of complimentary tickets.

His friends turn up at my house just to play ping-pong. His life fits me like a glove.

I tell Isabelle, "I have never been so happy."

But she's worried, and she's right. "Isn't it all a bit much though?" she asks, inarticulate, but accurate as ever.

"I don't know what you mean," I say.

She shrugs. "I don't know," she says. "It all just seems a bit ... unsustainable."

I have folded into this relationship and I'm disappearing fast.

Isabelle is right, it can't be sustained, but I can't do anything else. My own life is a big blurred mess, I don't know where I'm going or what I'm doing, so we live Hugo's life instead and it suits us both – one size fits all. I am so happy, so busy, so overflowing with joy that I can't even be bothered to think about the implications of any of this.

When summer arrives, Hugo has time off and we languish in bed until twelve. We walk in the forest; we diet together and drive to the mountains to buy more hens.

When we have dinner parties, some of my friends reappear, tempted to travel out to me by the chance to escape the heat and overcrowding of Nice in August. They seem to love Hugo almost as much as I do. "Try to keep this one a bit longer," they say.

I awaken in the mornings, snuggle to his back and he stretches, yawns and snuggles into me.

One morning in September, he rolls onto his back instead, stares at the ceiling. "How long have we been together now?" he asks sleepily.

I count. "Feb, March, April, May. Nine months," I say. *"Nearly nine months."*

Hugo moves away, it's barely perceptible, but he definitely moves away.

"Why?" I ask, propping myself up on one elbow.

He pauses a moment. "Does that mean that we're a couple?"

I can tell that this is multiple-choice. I know deep down, that it's a trick question, that there's a right answer and a wrong answer, and that the obvious answer may not be the correct one. I can sense that there's a lot to lose.

In panic, I go for honesty. "I suppose the fact that we've slept together almost every night for nine months could imply that we're a couple, yeah. So? What's wrong?"

Hugo says, "Hm."

He gets up; he dresses. Saying, "Sorry, but I need some space today," he leaves without eating breakfast.

I sit and wait.

Isabelle says, "C'est normale!" "A break after nine months is normal. Just give him some space."

"But is it just a break?" I wonder. *"Let it just be a break,"* I pray.

A week drones by, I give him space. The emptiness in my house is overpowering, as if everything is frozen, everything is on hold.

I swear even the plants stop growing.

I sit and wait and bite my nails.

Hugo has taken everything: the friends, the cuddles, the sex, the laughter. It's still summer, but I can't be bothered to do anything, so I sit indoors waiting.

It feels like winter.

It takes two weeks for him to get his thoughts together.

One afternoon I glance out into the garden and he's there stroking the cat. I run out to him, run *at* him. "Thank God!" I say.

But the expression on his face tells all: panic and pain. "I'm sorry," he says. "I don't understand myself, but I... I guess I need a break, I need time to think."

"I thought we *had* a break," I say. "I thought that's what we were doing."

His eyes shine, his hands are trembling. "A month," he says. "Give me a month to work out what's going on."

He walks around the house, collects his remaining stuff and rides away.

I wait six weeks before I go to see him. He sits me down, holds my hand. "I'm sorry," he says, "but what we have, well it's not what I want."

I think of a line from Torch Song Trilogy, *"It's funny because it's what I dream of..."*

He hands me a bag with, "some things" of mine.

When I get home, I angrily empty the bag onto the bed. It contains every gift I ever gave him, oh and my spare toothbrush. The toothbrush makes me weep; the toothbrush strikes me as *really* final.

But deep down, I always think he'll come back.

I'll guess I'll always expect that call.

20-20 Vision

I drag through the classic trauma cycle, only this time it takes longer than usual. Denial: he'll be back; it was just too wonderful. Anger: I bet the bastard's actually shagging someone else. Depression: toast, cigarettes, rosé and chocolate. Rebound: diet, swimming pool, gym, reading the personals all over again.

These are promising as always, so I answer a couple, but it's the usual mirage in the desert, lots of guys who sound hopeful, who seem even better in the contact email, but who when I call them either say, "Come around now, I'm nude and waiting with my throbbing tool in my hand," or "Yeah I really like your voice, I'd like to meet you tomorrow, and hey, if it all goes well we could we live together!" If all else fails then, the voice, when I call, sounds like Tinky Winky on ecstasy.

I will not get depressed, I will not give in, I will survive. I will, yet again bounce back.

I force myself to go to the pub, to attend bike club meetings, secretly hoping to see Hugo again or if not, another, better Hugo. Could such a thing exist?

The night I meet Laurent I am drinking with friends from the bike club outside La Rusca. The bikes are lined up along the pavement.

Jean-Paul says, "Mark, meet Laurent."

Laurent smiles at me, and Jean-Paul moves away. I can tell that he's dumping him on me but I think, *Cute* and I think, *Young*.

Laurent grins, smiles, winks and moves to my side.

When we move on to a restaurant, Laurent sticks with us, sticks to my side. He is gushing, enthusiastic; he stares at me with huge brown eyes. He asks me what bike I have, tells me that he loves motorbikes and that he loves bikers. I smile at him indulgently.

Around eleven p.m. he says, "I'd *love* to go out with a biker like you."

I make my excuses and escape.

Over the next two weeks he pursues me by all means, low and high tech combined. I get postcards, telephone calls, emails and SMS messages. Jean-Paul calls me as go-between to tell me that Laurent is "desperate" to see me again.

I ask him why he dumped him on me in the first place.

"No reason really. He's nice," he insists. "He's just a bit, well, *clingy.*"

"I KEEP THINKING ABOUT U," says an SMS, "CALL ME!"

The truth is that I do like him; he's very cute, relaxed and funny, in a twenty-year-old kind of way. I wonder myself why I don't go for it.

It's the age thing, but why should the idea worry me so?

I discuss the dilemma with gay friends who ask me how old he is and wince as they calculate the difference. They say, "Why not, but what would you have in common?" or, "Well the ancient Greeks did it, but then we're not ancient Greeks, *are* we?" At the same time they egg me on. "And *do* call me and tell me what happens if you do," they say excitedly.

Laurent is ever present, ever persistent.

One Friday I phone my oldest straight friend, Steve. He's flabbergasted. "But I thought you were supposed to be immoral sex machines, endlessly shagging everything in sight," he says. "I thought it was easy for you guys, I thought that was the whole *point.*"

"Not the *whole* point, surely?" I say.

"Well if *I* was single and met a cute twenty year-old bird who was up for it I wouldn't hesitate for a second," he says. His demonic laugh reveals it as complete truth.

I *like* this advice, so I call a couple of other straight male friends. They unanimously *would* have sex with a twenty year old, and their enthusiasm is such that I suspect they probably wouldn't mind doing it together. They are all shocked that the idea should present me with any kind of moral dilemma. "The guy is an adult for God's sake," they say.

It's true. *"He does have a beard,"* I think.

In the end of course the hormones win, I go with the straights. I like to have opposing advice; it lets me do what I like and still feel justified.

So I drag little Laurent into my lair and it's not so difficult.

The first week goes fine, in a vanilla kind of a way. He has no real opinions on anything, so it feels a bit like trying to read an empty exercise book. But he's always in a good mood, always willing to do anything, and for once his homosexuality seems to pose him no problem at all. His friends at college know, his parents know. *"A different generation,"* I think.

I lie in bed watching him sleep: his face looks lovely. He always smiles as he sleeps, sometimes he actually laughs as he dreams.

I ponder the fact that the gays I know these days have more hang-ups about sex than their straight equivalents. I wonder if we thirty-somethings haven't gone from defining our sex lives *in spite* of what others may care to think about us, to defining them in the *very hope* of disproving what we worry others *might* think about us. As far as Laurent is concerned no one actually seems to care enough to think about us at all.

I wake up one morning next to him. He's sleeping soundly and as I lie there I wonder if the sex will get any better – he never seems to actually move very much. I think, *"Whatever, this is fine."*

As I stroke his bare shoulder, he wakes up, stretches animal-like then turns and hugs me.

He says, "I love you."

I cough. I say, "That's nice, but you might want to slow down there."

He says, "But I *know*. I really *love* you."

I go to make tea and he follows me to the kitchen. He's nude and his dick stands out at ninety degrees.

I look at him, slim and fit and youthful. I don't remember *ever* having a physique like that. "What sport do you do to have a body like that?" I ask him.

He grins at me; he shrugs. "I don't," he says. "I'm naturally muscly."

"Typical," I say, stirring the tea.

He says, "So can I come and live here?" The question comes out naturally – apparently, a waking, logical, obvious thought.

I turn to frown at him. I shake my head. "Absolutely," I say. "Not!"

"But it does make sense," he argues.

"We've been seeing each other a little over a week," I say.

"Nearly two weeks," says Laurent. "Anyway, my friend Josette moved in with her boyfriend after a week. Now they're getting married."

I stare at him. I shake my head. "Laurent!" I say, "It's *not* gonna happen."

He frowns at me; he goes a little red. He looks angry, upset, and his eyes start to shine.

I know that this won't last and I wonder, *"Why not?"* When did the relationship game all get so heavy, so weighted, so complicated? When did it become impossible to just say, "Sure, why not?"

Mobile Fantasy

Even the way it starts is strange, a simple text message on my mobile phone, a message to call Jean-Luc. Jean-Luc – the cute one, the guy I have been bumping into infrequently for nearly ten years, every time with a different boyfriend in tow. Jean-Luc who always seems pleased to have a coffee with me but nothing more.

Jean-Luc has the kind of charm that people recruiting salesmen dream of, that flirty way of giving you his complete attention, of staring deep into your eyes with a cocky smile, whether you're his landlady or his prey.

I phone him immediately. I guess he needs instructions on how to get to Isabelle's party, or maybe someone's phone number.

When he asks me to dinner, I am more than surprised.

Jean-Luc has changed. He's still beautiful; he still has those big brown eyes and the little smile lines emanating from them, and he still asks endless streams of questions. But he no longer listens to the replies. Most of the time I can't even finish the phrase before he interrupts me with the next question. *"Maybe he was always like that and I didn't notice,"* I think.

I wonder what I am doing here, but in a very detached kind of way, as though I am reading a story, as though it is unfolding before me one page at a time, I am intrigued – an actor in my own life. So I accept the invitation to his flat just to see what will happen.

What happens is that we have frigid, sterile, dull sex. Afterwards – and it doesn't take long – I leave feeling more bored than cheap.

The next day he calls me again, he wants me to spend another night with him.

When I say, as kindly as I can, "No, sorry, but this isn't working for me," he breaks down and weeps into the phone. Luckily he can't see my surprised grimace.

"I'm sorry, I should have told you," he explains. His sister is dying – cancer. He can't think of anything else, he's not usually like this; he *wasn't* listening to anything I said. "I couldn't even concentrate when we were having sex," he says.

The conversation floods on and on and on until I feel saturated. I am interrupted by a knock on the door and so I promise, out of kindness, to visit him later that evening.

Back in his flat, he tells me the whole story. She's in the terminal stages of leukaemia and he's leaving tomorrow to stay with her until the end. He needs me to stay with him tonight. "I've got no right to ask you this but I'm asking you anyway," he pleads.

So I stay.

He grips my arm as he sleeps a deep tormented sleep. I lie looking at the patterns the blinds make on his ceiling, listening to the passing cars, wondering why I'm doing this, wondering if anyone *wouldn't* do this for a fellow human being.

In the morning he's sullen but grateful, and I am tired. I take him to the airport.

The text messages start an hour after he arrives.

"I MISS U. I WISH WE COULD BE TOGETHER" This is surreal enough to start to interest me intellectually; strange enough to make me follow through, just to see where this will go.

Day by day, by telephone and by text message I follow the death of a woman I have never met, the sister of a man I barely know.

"SHES HAVING TR BREATHING. I NEED YOUR ARMS AROUND ME."

The next day, "SHES ON VENTILATOR. WE DISCUSS WHO LOOKS AFTER KIDS."

Then, "THEY'VE STOPPED THE DRUGS... I THINK IS THE END." And, "HER EX IS HERE SHE HATES HIM. V DIFFICULT. I MISS YOU"

Finally, exactly a week later, the chapter ends, "THATS IT ITS OVER. PLEASE CALL."

Robotically, at three a.m. I counsel him over the phone; he needs to know that I will be there for him when he returns. Dishonestly I assure him that I will; I think he needs that answer.

I don't love him; strangely I don't think I even *like* him – he strikes me as dishonest and hysterical and selfish. *"But,"* I reason, *"who wouldn't be under these circumstances?"*

I follow the preparations for the funeral, the negotiation of the inheritance, the visits to the notary. I get confused and think I'm following a radio play.

Friends seem confused as well and ask me for the latest instalment, but this play is real life, it actually moves me to tears.

It makes me sad with the loneliness of my role, of his role, of the whole plot.

Two days before he returns, I have to go away to England. My own brother Peter is in intensive care with a burst appendix.

Everyone says he should be OK, but my mother says he could die.

"You just can't tell with a burst appendix," she says, as ever, the prophet of doom.

"*Synchronicity,*" I think. "*Maybe it's a sign.*" But a sign of what?

During my trip, Jean-Luc's SMS messages dry up. I resist the temptation to keep him posted on Peter's illness and he doesn't seem interested anyway; he's had enough to deal with, I tell myself.

I spend Christmas in the hospital trying to make conversation. Peter and I know virtually nothing about each other's lives, but we still can't think of much to tell each other.

By the time he's out of danger, over a week has gone by and it's nearly New Year's Eve. I think about staying, going to some major bash in a London nightclub for a change. But when I phone Jean-Luc he says, "Oh, please come back... it'd be so good to spend the New Year together. And we haven't seen each other for nearly six weeks after all."

I'm actually having a little trouble remembering what he looks like. Of course, I remember vaguely. I remember individual features – I've known him for years, but I can't quite picture the whole thing, can't quite piece them together in my mind's eye.

In my letterbox back in Grasse, I find two free tickets to the Cannes dance festival for the thirtieth of December – they're from Hugo.

I phone Jean-Luc and he's charming. "Brilliant!" he says. "I'd love to go."

He asks me to pick him up early. "That way we'll have time for a drink beforehand," he enthuses.

When he opens the door I can see that he's himself again, he looks fine. He steps back from me, appraising me as one might look at a painting. I wouldn't be surprised if he half closed his eyes to better appreciate the tones.

I say, "Me voilà!" and wave the tickets at him with a grin.

He frowns at me.

I frown back. "What?" I ask.

He pauses. "I'm sorry," he says.

I wrinkle my brow. "Sorry?"

He nods. "I've been an arsehole. This whole thing has been a mistake. I wasn't myself, I thought I... I thought I loved you, but well, I wasn't myself, and I'm sorry, but I got over it I guess. I'm really sorry."

I wrinkle my nose and say, "Uh?"

"Would you be hurt if we just forgot this ever happened?"

I am flabbergasted. As I stand in silence staring at him, I realise for the first time in my life the true meaning of *flabbergasted*.

For some reason he repeats himself, only this time more slowly, changing the emphasis. "I wasn't *myself*. I'm sorry, would you be *hurt* if we just *forget* this ever happened?" As he says "this", he points between himself and me.

I realise he thinks that I haven't understood. I stare at him and slightly shake my head. "You're completely mad!" I say.

"I'm sorry!" He repeats.

For some reason my anger focuses on the wasted tickets to the dance festival; I wave them at him. "And what about *these? Arsehole!"* I say.

As I drive to Cannes I feel stupid and ugly and rejected and worthless. I want to have a good cry for myself, but it will have to wait till I get home. I can't let the tickets go to waste.

I try to give one ticket away to the stupid, suspicious people who are queuing to pay, but they look at me as if I am mad, then stare at the floor to avoid the absolute *terror* of a free ticket.

I angrily leave it on the counter and, after a few seconds, more than one person makes a grab for it. But no one thanks me. It wasn't my ticket once I put it down, I suppose.

The dance starts, and it's beautiful.

Ten minutes in, I see Hugo spring onto the stage. Even disguised as a tree I know it's him.

It brings me to tears, different tears.

And I know I'll get over Jean-Luc long before I get over Hugo.

Avignon

It is New Year's Eve and I am so completely depressed I have stopped moving. The episode with Jean-Luc has left me feeling dreadful... The dance yesterday was wonderful, but I ended up going for drinks with Hugo afterwards which did nothing to help. He danced like a dream, and of course he was lovely to me, but the only kind of relationship I want with Hugo is the kind we had.

I never was very good at ex-boyfriends, or New Year's Eves for that matter. This one is looking to be the worst on record. *"Oh how I should have stayed in England, how ridiculous to have come back to spend it with Jean-Luc,"* I think.

I drag myself from my bed and make a cup of thick black coffee. The whisky bottle on the kitchen counter reminds me why I am feeling so shocking.

One by one I call all my friends, but as I'm too embarrassed to explain my desperation, they casually tell me that it's a bit late. Everyone has restaurants booked, parties to go to, train, plane or bus tickets to get away.

I build a fire, set up the computer in front of it. The cat watches me.

"We're going to do some shopping on the Internet," I tell her.

I connect to a chat site, sort the list of people to show only those living on the Côte D'Azur. The cat half-heartedly raises a paw, taps at the pointer moving across the screen.

My screen flashes almost immediately; I click on the icon.

His nickname is *Flash*. In the photo he's sitting astride a Yamaha R1 motorbike. *"Another biker!"* I think. *"How many gay bikers can there be out there?"*

He opens with, "Hi Biker, what's the story?"

We discuss bikes; we discuss work – he's an architect.

We discuss New Year – he too is depressed; his boyfriend split up with him a week ago and he hasn't the heart to party tonight.

He sends me another picture, this time without crash helmet, standing next to his bike, an unmistakable bulge in the front of his jeans. He types, "What are you into?"

I yawn. "Sleep," I reply. "I'm going back to bed." I realise I just can't be bothered.

He types, "Not yet! Why not come to Avignon? We can get depressed together."

I thank him; I refuse. Avignon is three hours away and it is five degrees and drizzling outside. My car won't start; I know – I tried it this morning. I disconnect.

Owen phones from Australia, wishes me a happy New Year. I can hear people laughing in the background. He forgets and asks me if I'm spending it with Hugo, then corrects himself to Jean-Luc.

I tell him that that too is over. I realise from his voice that he's not even surprised, that my love life doesn't even register on his sympathy scale anymore. He says, "Well don't spend it on your own, that's the worst thing you can do, and don't forget, we love you."

I hate the *we*, it sounds diluted. I suppose it should be more – being loved by both of them – but it strikes me as less. Jealousy I suppose. By the time I hang up I am morbidly miserable. As I stare into the fire a tear dribbles from my eye.

I walk around the cold damp garden and I wonder if I should go to Avignon. The rain has stopped but the temperature is dropping and the roads are wet.

"They'll probably be icing over soon," I think.

When I come back in, even the log fire is having trouble displaying any enthusiasm. I sit on a stool in front of it, blow on it, and fan it with a magazine, but the remaining flames flicker and die. The wood must be wet. It all wells up in me. Hugo and Jean-Luc and poor, poor Mark.

I cry for New Year's Eves past, present and future. I imagine myself seventy years old, still alone with the cat. I realise my cat will die before then and I cry some more – pathetic self-pitying sobs.

I phone up my closest friends in Nice and try to sound perky, try to force my way into their *soirées*, but at five in the afternoon there is really no way; it just can't be done.

I think of friends in England who would never find it impossible to see me, to let me join them, and I phone them instead. They're too far away to be able to help and ask me in concerned tones if I am, "going to be all right?"

As I wonder what they mean, I realise. I think, *"Maybe I won't."*

Maybe one day it will all just be too much for me. Maybe, if I stay here staring at the wet garden with my cat while the whole world is celebrating a new millennium – maybe that day will be today.

I connect back to the chat and *Flash* is still there; he sends me a message immediately: "Changed your mind I hope?"

"If I don't I may just kill myself." It's a terrifying thought. I type, "Yes."

"Really?" he replies.

"Yes," I type. "I'm coming. Send me directions."

The roads are deserted.

I am wearing thermal underwear, jogging trousers and sweatshirt, jeans, and motorcycle leathers. I look like a pumped up Darth Vader.

I feel ecstatic and optimistic; I have seized my own destiny, and whatever happens in Avignon, it can't be worse than the alternative. Flash has agreed that there will be no obligations and he has promised me a great restaurant this evening.

Ten minutes into the journey the daylight fades away, my visor starts to steam up, my fingers go numb.

As I move onto the *autoroute,* it starts to drizzle. My gloves soak up the rain, the wind and rushing air turn my fingers to senseless blocks, but still I am happy. Proof that the answer to depression, as my little self-help book says, is indeed, "Do something. *Anything!*"

Half an hour from Avignon, I push through ten minutes of torrential rain. I should pull off under a bridge, see if it stops, but I daren't interrupt the momentum.

As the rain works its way down into my boots, my feet start to freeze as well. It soaks through my scarf, and starts to dribble down my back. It forms a puddle between my legs and soaks up into my arse.

By the time I reach the exit I feel desolate, numb and frankly ridiculous. I stand in a brightly lit callbox and phone him, my teeth chattering. He answers, says he's on his way.

I jump up and down in the callbox to warm up – my boots squelch.

I watch the rain drift past the sodium street lamps, watch it ease off.

People in warm, glowing cars sweep past, peer at me through misty windows.

After twenty minutes, I phone him again, but of course there is no answer. After forty minutes, I start to flick through the yellow pages, miserably eyeing up hotel options. I feel like crying again, a night alone in a cheap hotel could actually be worse than dinner with the cat.

Then suddenly there is the roar of a perforated silencer and he pulls up. He's wearing one-piece racing leathers. He lifts his visor, bangs his petrol tank.

"Sorry, they were all closed. You OK?" He holds out a hand.

I shrug. I wring out a glove to show how wet I am. "Flash I presume," I say shaking his hand.

"Jean-Luc actually," he laughs. "Let's go get you changed."

I sigh. *"Not Jean-Luc,"* I think. *"Anything but Jean-Luc."*

We head into Avignon. We shout at each other at sets of traffic lights.

He shouts, "You looked thinner in the photo!"

I shout, "Clothes, lots! Still frozen though."

We drive around the walls of Avignon, sweep past the famous half bridge reflecting beautifully in the wet tarmac; we ride through one of the gates into the walled city, over cobblestones, and we have arrived.

We park the bikes in his garage and he kisses me on the cheek, says, "Bienvenue."

I see a set of handcuffs hanging with the tools. He follows my gaze and winks at me as a puddle forms around my feet. He pushes me though into the lounge. "Better get those clothes off," he says with a grin.

We never do make it to that restaurant.

The sex is rough and dirty.

Jean-Luc hardly removes his leathers the whole weekend – they turn him on, and I don't mind myself. He looks a bit overweight without them.

We have nothing really in common, so we don't really talk. It's all pointless and base. But at the stroke of midnight I'm not only alive, but I come for the third time, which, it has to be said, is better than watching the cat watch the fire go out.

Barbie Boy

It starts with an email – a photo of a taut muscular body with a grin, crescent shaped blue eyes with a twinkle. The accompanying words are rounded, intelligent friendly. "I saw your ad, and though I hate motorbikes, I've got nothing against bikers, and it is, at least, a method of transport. Why not use it to come and meet me for coffee?"

I send back an email: chatty, warm, but stuffed with questions.

Twenty-four hours later the replies arrive. His name is Thomas, he's thirty-eight, an ex ice-skater. I try not to think of sequined leotards.

He works in Cannes in public relations. He likes cinema, reading, theatre, walking. He hates nightclubs, motorbikes and Celine Dion.

He sounds almost perfect. Hating Celine Dion almost makes up for not liking motorbikes, in my book, at least.

I hastily type my reply and propose a meeting this evening, in Cannes, at *Hype*.

I move the cursor over the send button, but something makes me hesitate. I push the mouse gently away from me, delicately, as one might a bomb. I frown at the screen, and move to the kitchen to make myself a coffee.

When I return, I sip my coffee and re-read his email, re-read my reply. This time, I notice the signature at the bottom of his message. The man has his own web site – I click on the link.

The welcome page is fluorescent pink. It is covered with animated icons: dogs wag tails, letters post themselves, smilies smile, a jack-in the box springs out. After a few seconds the music starts, a simplified, one finger version of Gloria Gaynor's, *I Will Survive*.

I cringe and click on *Photos*. I see Thomas hugging all his friends and I see Thomas wearing a Mexican sombrero. I click on, *What I like best*.

I read, *Little House on the Prairie, Julia Roberts, Boney M*. I read *Barbie*. I giggle.

Barbie is a link so I click on it – there are more photos of Barbie than there are of Thomas.

I have a collection of over a hundred Barbie dolls and twenty-four Kens, the text reads. *When people ask me why I like Barbie I have trouble explaining, but here goes: for me Barbie and Ken represent an ideal. Barbie is beautiful, successful, loved. Her couple is an ideal too. Barbie and Ken are very much in love. They are thin and beautiful and well dressed.*

143

They have been together for years. I would like to feel as perfect as Barbie as I walk down the street with my very own Ken!

I grind my teeth and drink a second cup of coffee before replying.

"Sorry Thomas," I type.
"I looked at your web site and I guess I don't think I could ever be anyone's Ken. I hate Barbie because "she", sorry that would be "it", is in fact a garish plastic child's toy made in China.
Sorry, all the best.
Mark."

It seems mean, but it strikes me that this guy really needs to get a life. *"Maybe no one has ever told him,"* I think.

Half an hour later I have his reply. It lasts a couple of pages but ends with, *"You are a narrow-minded, judgmental, rude, ignorant idiot. Well I hope you've had fun, I can imagine you laughing at me, imagine you telling your friends all about it. I am so glad to have been of service. If our paths should ever cross please don't bother to say hello."*

I laugh, I think, *"OK, suits me fine."*
I make a resolution: No more Internet. Never again!
With a couple of exceptions, I stick to it.

Groove

The music throbs, rolls, crashes over us. Miss Honey, the guest DJ behind glass, frenetically slides new vinyl over the third turntable, pushes her lips out, grooves with the pleasure of the mix. She nods her head, rocks the disc lining up the beat, releases it into the atmosphere. She closes her eyes, rolls her head from side to side and breaks into a grin as the saxophone adds itself to the ambient funk. She's too tall, too black, too lippy – too woman to be woman.

The crowd is heaving, thumping – the dance floor rocks and rolls beneath the feet. Some are aerobic, angular; some Latino and sexy; others are flailing, screaming as the music climaxes, crashes to the ground. A black guy to my left is grooving, rolling, spinning.

For some it's a serious affair, lips jut out, eyebrows frown.

I close my eyes, rock backwards and forwards and lose myself in it all.

Miss Honey pulls a slider down to zero, leaves us frustrated, the dance floor a wasteland of rhythm without bass. The music builds, the rhythm transforms, becomes faster. A voice rises, climbs above the treble, "take it, take it, take it," it screams. The cymbals become harsher, louder, the voice mounts. The small guy opposite me gyrates his hips in small tight circles, bites his lip, eyes open, eyebrows lifted in expectation.

Tiny hints of the baseline sneak through to the speakers, the music builds to its climax, "Take it a-l-l t-h-e w-a-y," laughs the voice.

Miss Honey whacks in the bass and we are drowned by the hugeness of it. The black guy spins three-sixty degrees; the small guy opposite breaks into a huge relieved grin. My spine tingles. I close my eyes, grin, swoop and fall on the melody.

Someone behind me falls against my back, barges me forward and I open my eyes just as I bash into the small guy. He catches me, grins at me and winks.

I watch him dance – the same tight little movements, easy, no pretence, dancing for himself. He stares into my eyes, ecstatic. *"On ecstasy probably,"* I think.

We grin, we roll, we move closer. The crowd pushes us; we let it happen. From time to time when our arms brush, electric arcs leap across.

He moves away and I dance, follow his movements, follow the back of his blue sweatshirt through the crowd, down to the end, off to the right hand bar.

I push off to the left, take another route and end up accidentally-on-purpose by his side. He shouts his order over to the barman, then turns and performs an exaggerated double take at me.

He points behind him at the DJ. "She is sooo good," he shouts.

I nod.

"Beer?" he asks.

I nod. "Beer!"

We move to an upstairs bar where we have to shout less. His name is Fabian, he's very thin and he has thinning hair. He's not really good looking, but when he smiles his face lights up, radiates joy, and he smiles all the time.

We talk, then we dance again. We roll and bounce against each other until Miss Honey quits the box at four a.m.

Fabian nods towards the door, I follow him.

"Where do you live?" he asks.

"Grasse," I say.

"Jesus that's a long way!" He strokes the side of my face with his hand.

"I can take you," I say nodding eagerly. "I can bring you back tomorrow."

He grins at me. "I have a car," he says. "I'll follow."

As I drive, I glance in the mirror at the white Fiat following.

I wonder if I am in love, if it is possible. We haven't really spoken; we haven't really met. We have only danced; we have only kissed. So not love then.

"Then what is this fluttering at the top of my chest?" I wonder.

At home I open the French windows. We lounge on the sofa, look out at the night; the first summer light is coming over the horizon. Birds are singing prematurely in the trees.

We drink tea and Fabian looks through my CD's. He says, "Oh, *I* have this," and, "cool, Kid Loco," and, "is this one any good? I don't think I know it."

We lie on the sofa, his head on my chest, and I stroke his hair. I think we should be getting down to sex before we fall asleep, but this is so nice, so much closer to what I need. He tells me about his parents, his job, his dog.

My cat bounds in from her night-hunt and settles on his lap. I smile, I am happy. I watch him upside down as he talks, feel the vibrations of his soft Bordeaux accent in my stomach. He's beautiful, gentle and honest and open.

Eventually, around seven-thirty a.m. he says, "I'm tired." Sunlight creeps across the lawn.

"We should sleep," I say.

"I like you," he says in my arms as we doze off. "It's weird."

"Why weird?" I ask.

"I feel safe," he says, "as though nothing bad can happen to me."

I smile. "It can't," I say.

We wake up together, entangled and sweaty. We lie watching the afternoon sun force through the gaps in the shutters.

I kiss his neck. "Hello you," I say.

He sighs, turns, and looks at me with big brown eyes. "Hi," he says.

I hug him tightly. "Great evening!" I say.

There is a silence. His body tightens. "I'm HIV positive," he says. "Sorry."

I say nothing. I sigh. I hug him a bit tighter.

"You're not then?"

"No." The words catch in my throat.

He pulls my arms tighter around him. "Oh well," he says.

I sigh.

He shrugs. "Another story that won't work then."

I sigh. "Who knows?"

I pause. I think back. I remember what friends have told me, the paranoia of infection, the anguish of feeling you're not allowed to get angry, not allowed to be demanding about anything, not with someone who might die.

"I've done it before, too complicated," he says, "too much stress, too much paranoia."

"I know. It wouldn't be easy," I say.

He rolls away onto his back. "Nah," he says. "Been there, done that, I don't even want to try."

"We could see how it goes?" I say. I stare at him; my eyes sting.

He shrugs. "Nah," he says, sitting up. "You can make me breakfast though; I'm starving."

We eat; we talk. We lounge in the hammock until sunset, then I close the door to the little white Fiat.

He winds down the window; big brown eyes look up at me. "Thanks," he says, "you're lovely."

I smile at him, a lump in my throat. "So are you. I'll, um, see you in the club then?"

He nods; he smiles. His eyes shine, and with a little wave he drives away.

André

I pull up on the crunchy gravel, flip down the side-stand and pull off my crash helmet. I walk to the small group standing at the side of the road. Everyone is wearing wet weather gear, shiny and colourful. I look around – I think we all look pretty sexy.

Jean-Paul, our secretary introduces two new members to me. The first is a pneumatic blonde from Marseilles, her name is Laurence and she has a broad smile, an amazing cat-woman waist and a bust that fills her motorcycle leathers. She's with her girlfriend – ninety kilos, frizzy straw hair, dark roots, and eyebrows painted in too high.

I say, "Bonjour." I look at the couple standing side by side. *"Why?"* I wonder.

Jean-Paul introduces me to another member, André.

André is the male equivalent of Laurence, except with no apparent partner in tow, one metre eighty, broad sporty shoulders, bright generous smile, shaved head, goatee beard. He shakes my hand, looks me up and down. He's wearing leather jeans and a grey nylon motorcycle jacket, my sight lingers on the drops of rain clinging to his thigh.

We stand, we chat and drink dreadful coffee from *Quick*.

Jean-Paul winks at me as he tells me that André works as a sports masseur. We stamp our feet and watch our breath rise into the cold January air until it is time to leave.

Riding through the winding greenery of the Var, I'm having trouble with the bends. I'm spending too much time looking at André's back, at his rear, at his shiny thighs; I have to force myself to look at the road.

When we stop at traffic lights I pull up beside him.

He shouts, "Beautiful road!"

I nod and give him a thumbs-up.

He shouts, "No rain!"

In the restaurant in St Tropez he sits next to me.

We laugh about the dreadful pizza. André removes his jacket – his t-shirt is white and tight and his arms are covered in swirls of dark hair. We talk about our likes: biking, camping, music, dancing. We agree on all our dislikes too: Caviar, snobby restaurants, fundamentalist non-smoking non-drinking Christians.

I am seduced by our similarities.

I know that all relationships start with the search for similarity, I also know that they all end with the affirmation of difference.

I wonder vaguely if that's what we're doing, starting a relationship.

We ride back along the coast, around the red rocky cliffs, alongside the impossibly blue Mediterranean. As the sun fades we start to chill; my nose is cold, my fingers iced. I invite everyone back to my place for a drink. Half come and half have other things to do, other people to see. André comes.

I light a log fire in the lounge and serve mulled wine to everyone except André who wants vodka. We sit, hands cupped in front of the fire – the red flickering makes everyone look beautiful, even Laurence's girlfriend.

The girls head off, they have a two hour drive to get home.

Fabrice downs a second mulled wine, drags himself wearily to his feet and follows them out.

André fills his glass with vodka; I look on approvingly. Apparently he's not intending leaving so soon.

Jean-Paul nudges his boyfriend and winks at me. They get up and say goodbye; I follow them out. "He's cute," says Jean-Paul. "And single."

I look nervously behind me. "Thanks," I say. "I worked that out for myself." He winks at me again. They climb onto his Suzuki, bump off down the track and I close the gate.

When I get back André is downing the last of his drink, crouching in front of the fire, poking at the logs. "That was *such* a good day," he says. The flames flicker across his face. He sounds slightly drunk and I glance at the bottle of vodka – half of it has gone.

We sit down on the sofa and André reaches forward, sloshes another four centimetres of vodka into his glass. "I really enjoyed today," he says. The slur in his voice is distinctive. He swigs at the glass and puts a hand on my leg as he speaks.

"Yeah it was great," I say, "but you should slow down a bit with the vodka."

He shrugs at me; he looks annoyed. "Merci Mama," he says. He downs the remains of his glass in single shot and laughs, pretends to throw the glass over his shoulder, Russian style.

I smile tightly. "Seriously though. You're not going to be able to drive otherwise."

He frowns at me; stares blearily into my eyes. "If I wanted my mother here, I would have brought her," he says.

I stand and force a little smile at him. "I think I'll make some coffee," I say nodding my head.

"Anyway," he says. "Who the fuck says I'm leaving anyway? Maybe I want to stay, maybe..." His voice peters out.

I look at him. I can see him wobbling out of control, like a spinning top at the end of the spin. I lift the bottle from the coffee table. "Sure," I say, "I'll just, erm, make that coffee all the same."

He grabs the base of the bottle, pulls it from my grip and plonks it back down on the coffee table. He grabs my hand, pulls me towards him.

I shake him loose, glare at him. "OK André, enough," I say.

His top lip curls. "What the fuck is wrong with you?" he asks.

"You need coffee, and then you need to go home," I say.

André shrugs theatrically. "Why?"

I stare him in the eye. "Because I'm telling you to," I say.

He jumps unsteadily to his feet. "Waste of fucking time," he says. He picks up his keys from the mantelpiece.

I shake my head. I touch his arm. "André, have some coffee, you've had too much..."

"Oh fuck off," he says, pushing me away, hard – I stumble backwards. "I know when I'm not welcome. Christ, it's worse than at home." He stumbles, trips on the coffee table; swipes his crash helmet from the floor.

"André?" I plead.

When he turns, his eyes are blazing and his face is puce. "I don't want your fucking coffee!" he says. "Got it?"

I nod. "Got it," I say.

He turns, opens the front door, and sweeps dramatically out slamming it behind him.

I raise a hand to my forehead, run it up through my hair and take a deep breath. "Not my problem," I say to myself, shaking my head.

I hear him start the engine. I hear a crash. I hear him say, "Merde!"

I open the front door in time to see him remounted and riding away. The gate lies on the ground, dented, unhinged, dead. A piece of plastic from his headlight lies beside it.

I snort in amazement and sit down on the doorstep. I smoke a cigarette and then cross the garden and lift the iron gate back onto its metal hinges – it no longer closes completely.

Back in the house I find André's gloves on the coffee table, but the bottle of vodka has gone.

Red T-Shirt

The Klub is packed for the "World famous" Jeff Mills but the music in my car on the way here was more danceable than Jeff's thumping rattle so I concentrate on the local fauna instead, vaguely hoping to catch sight of Fabien. On the stairs I bump into Yves, and we pretend we never fell out and shout at each other for a while.

A cute thirty year old with a shaved-head, biker-thing going is heading down the stairs in a skinny red t-shirt, only he's not looking where he's going, he's looking at yours truly, his head swivelling like a radar tracking-device as he moves.

When he reaches the last step, just before he spins into the dancers, he breaks into a grin. I have a double heartbeat.

"Did you see?" shouts Yves.

I nod wide-eyed.

"He was looking at you, not me, *right?*"

I nod again.

"Go!" laughs Yves, pushing me down the stairs.

It's almost impossible to move and by the time I catch up with Red T-shirt he has given up on me ever following and is heading back. As we sail past each other caught in different tides, he is momentarily squashed against my chest. "So packed!" he says, grinning up at me. The crowd carries him on.

The Klub is organised in a loop, so I carry on in the hope of squashing into him next time around, this time determined to seize the day.

I fight my way across the dance floor and up the stairs but when I get to the balcony, I see him dancing on the floor below with a heavy-set body-builder.

Yves, who is flailing around behind them, sees me and points, shrugging, mouthing, "What are you doing?"

I take a deep breath and head back around the loop, through the excitable Italians, around the gaggle of girly-boys and across the sea of bare chested tattoos on the stairs, and there is Red T-Shirt, heading up towards me.

I calculate the currents, position myself correctly and wait. As he pushes in front of me he stops. "Hi! What's *your* name?" he asks.

"Mark," I say. The pressure to move on is building. People are pushing.

"Hum, you're not French," he laughs.

"And you?"

"Jean-Philippe," he replies.

"Very French," I say. "That your boyfriend you were dancing with?"

"Nah, just a friend," he says.

"Good," I say, "I'm glad."

He squeezes my arm, slides his hand down over my arse and lets the stream carry him onwards.

I stand bemused; I shake my head. I vaguely consider following.

But a new feeling grips me. I just can't be bothered.

I can't be bothered fighting my way through the crowd, can't be bothered playing the cruising game, can't be bothered chatting this guy up all night in the vague hope that... That what? That we'll spend a night together? Or maybe a week; maybe even a year? But where's the point in that? What's the point if you just don't believe anymore?

So, I get to go home alone.

Better Late

I frown at the screen.
I try to remember.
As I read the mail it slowly comes back.

Dear Mark.

Do you remember me, the sax man from Chicago?
Do you still have this email address?
If you do, I'm sorry it has been so long.
I never did get back to France last year. I got a job with a great jazz band,
Chicago Belle. We toured all over the States, spent lots of time in New York
and Los Angeles. How anyone can live their whole lives in such unfriendly
environments, architecturally speaking, is beyond me.
I lost your email address, and then, I admit it, I forgot about you.
Anyway, it all finally came to an end, and I moved, guess where to? Nice!
I have some friends here who are putting me up. We're going to busk all
summer and then see what happens.
I wonder if you're still here. I was copying my old address book into one of
those new electronic things someone gave me for Christmas and I came
across your email address, and I thought, I wonder?
So did you meet the man of your dreams? I didn't.
I had a relationship with a singer in New York but it all went horribly
wrong. Maybe I'll tell you about it all one day.
So, if you do get this, and you are still in the south of France, then drop me
a line. I suppose that's a lot of "ifs". You probably won't even see this.

All the best.

Steve.

PS. It has been what, two years? So I've joined a more recent photo.
As you can see I've given up on any pretence of having hair.
Still some find that sexy. Don't they?

I lean towards the screen. I peer at the photo. The same familiar
grin, I actually remember it from the previous photo.
   I smile at the smiling face, and then I catch myself. "For God's
sake," I say out loud. "You don't even know him."

Five Kisses From Start To Finish

We are sitting in a restaurant. Until today we have only swapped emails. I have seen photos of him, his full smiling lips, his brown eyes. I know the shape of his life and the shape of his mouth when he plays the sax. I have read his prose so I feel that I know some of his dreams and his terrors.

The rest I have imagined: these shoulders, the smile, the glint in the eye. And I have imagined the future, the feeling of his arms around me, the tenderness of the kiss and the joy of drinking coffee on a cold sunny morning while he plays saxophone in a nearby room.

Right now he is here, opposite me. And this time – finally – he is exactly as I imagined him.

"You are exactly as I imagined," he says smiling coyly.

"Did you ever see that Woody Allen film?" I ask. "The one where..."

I'm thinking of the one where Woody goes on a blind date, where the girl opens the door, and he asks if they can get the first kiss over and done with straight away, to avoid further embarrassment.

He knows which film I mean before I say it, and he understands why I'm mentioning it. He leans towards me. "I think he was right," he says.

I am terrified. A kiss can be so revealing, so disappointing, so grounding. A single kiss has the power to destroy a dream, but the kiss, that first kiss, is perfect.

The second is at the end of the evening.

My heart is swollen to bursting point with joy. All feelings of loneliness and abandon, all images of the meanness of existence have gone. The future holds only promise.

Four hours of astounding, immediate intimacy, of finishing each other's phrases, of roaring with laughter at our jokes and then looking around the restaurant at the surprised faces, and then laughing again like guilty children.

We stand in the chill night air. A spring breeze is blowing in from the sea, swirling my hair and filling our nostrils with iodine, promise of distant places and voyages to come.

I want him to walk with me, to stick to me, to sleep with me, but I also want him to resist, to respect the first-ness of this meeting. It has taken that long.

He leans in; the wind is pushed from between us. His lips touch mine, slowly, gently, respectfully, and I shiver from cold and sheer pleasure. My body is a tingling mass of cells, electrified and crying out for more. We hug and I feel the broadness of his shoulders, the softness of his jacket, and he's gone. I am left alone, slightly drunk, but warm with satisfaction and hope.

The third kiss is in the park – Albert Premier. The sky is grey, the grass is wet from recent rain. He has brought a gift, a CD, Cesaria Evoria, his favourite.

It's actually my current favourite as well; I already have it but I don't tell.

I have brought sandwiches – cheese and butter in thick baguettes.

Old people sit on the other benches. I look at them and fretfully realise that their presence means that we can't kiss.

When he leans towards me I forget them though. I can feel a crumb on his bottom lip. This time these aren't just mouths kissing but orifices probing and exploring. I can taste the butter in his mouth.

I want to stay in this embrace forever but I have to return to my job. Those who have noticed are staring. One old lady is smiling at us, her head held wistfully at an angle.

At work I stare straight through my computer screen, unable to maintain focus on the text before me. A colleague asks, "What's his name?"

I feel drugged, sensual, sleepy and strokeable – like a cat on a red armchair. I smile knowingly – I am desired by Steve.

The fourth is as I get into the car, and it's just a peck on the cheek.

A peck has no pretence; it says, I know you – I can just peck you on the cheek for no reason.

We drive along the coast to Agay where we sit at the base of the crumbling red cliffs. It is icy cold and he opens his coat and wraps it around me. His thick white jumper scratches my neck and his nose nuzzles into my hair.

We sit on a comfortable mattress of dried seaweed and stare at the sea and talk the rhythmic talk of lovers, words lapping as the waves roll in, phrases rolling around like tongues kissing, searching for the truest expression of self.

I know that today is the day; we both know. My overnight bag is in the old borrowed car; his saxophone is next to it.

"I'll play for you later," he says. "We'll stop somewhere quiet."

He smokes a cigarette and hands it to me; sharing that cigarette strikes me as intimate and wonderful.

Clouds fight their way towards us over the Alps. I push back against his chest, fold myself deeper into his being and a tiny tear squishes from the corner of my eye. It could just be the cold wind making my eyes water, but it isn't – it's the pain of letting myself hope.

We head along the coast road; waves are crashing against the rocks. The closed seaside towns seem desolate and beautiful.

At Fréjus we head up to the A8. As we thunder along the motorway it starts to drizzle. The car feels warm and safe and a silence falls upon us. To start with it is a comfortable silence.

We are both thinking about the joy of being able to do this – being able to simply go away for a weekend with someone and feel so comfortable.

But tension eases into the air. The rain gets harder, the light outside dimmer.

By Marseilles I am feeling walled in by a deafening vacuum. I don't know what it means. I look at him for reassurance, he turns; he smiles. He is perfect.

My hand is resting on his leg. I have to lift it when he changes gear, rupture and reconciliation over and over.

I feel sick with some unknown sentiment – I analyse it for meaning, try to compare it with stress, pre-sex nerves, love, but none of them seem to fit.

I am overcome by an inexplicable sadness, not a weary maudlin sadness but something huge and profound. I don't know where it comes from.

He fumbles behind us, pulls a cassette from his bag, and slips it into the player. He fiddles with the controls and it starts. It's Cesaria Evoria.

He leans across and kisses me, then looks back at the road. I know that I am in love, real love, like I was with Hugo, all over again. Who would have thought it possible?

I wonder if this time it can last, and decide that it actually doesn't matter.

I think of the Buddhist meditation on death I read this morning. For the first time I understand that it is possible to be ready. "Oh little bird, if now is the moment then that is fine, for I have lived and loved and I am ready."

I stretch, I smile at him and I feel his leg tense beneath my hand.

His expression changes muscle by muscle – I see it happen; see it ripple across his face. His forehead tightens, his eyes widen, his mouth drops.

It happens so slowly. I am torn between his face, so twisted, so distorted, so beautiful, and whatever he is seeing.

I glance in front. I see the tunnel, I see the road works, I see the truck.

There is no safe place, the car is skidding now, sluing sideways, and I am emptying.

A vast chasm of death is opening before me and I feel angry and cheated and alone, but then, just before we pile into the truck, in those last few microseconds, amazingly, as though someone had added a few extra seconds to the frame just for this moment, he turns slowly away from the road, turns to look at me, and through the terror I see the love.

And strangely, it's not the love that we feel for each other, but the love for every one of them, for every hug and every kiss, for family for friends, for lovers, for every shared moment of joy. It is huge and profound and enveloping.

It sucks and tugs and pulls us in.

Epilogue

I climb out of my brother's car. "Will you be OK?" he asks me. Brighton's sea sparkles with sunlight behind his head. I nod. "Sure!"

I force a smile. As I turn to face the street I hear him drive away. In truth I am possessed by terror: terror of the outside world, terror of how people other than nurses will react to the scar, the sling, the limp.

Terror of ever trying again to find happiness, of having to live when I thought it was all over and done with – of having to live with what-might-have-beens, of having to do all this again, when the end had turned out to be so easy, so relaxing, so beautiful.

I start to walk slowly up the hill towards the Laines.

It's a sunny day – blue skies, a gentle wind – but I can feel no joy. I feel scared and desperate and shaky. Tears are pushing behind my eyes, I squint to stop them coming out.

I walk past a multicoloured terrace of guesthouses.

On a balcony a carpenter works bare-chested; he is tanned and absorbed in his work. I pause for a moment to rest my leg and watch him sand the handrail.

As I start to walk again he stops and looks down at me.

He pauses, a gentle smile spreads slowly across his lips. His eyes are warm, compassionate. He winks, then slowly turns back and continues his sanding.

I gulp. I step sideways and lean on the wall beside me.

It is nothing but a smile from a stranger; but a smile is a smile, and a smile is a sign. A door has creaked open, and emotion is rushing through the crack.

Tears roll down my cheeks.

And I realise that I might be OK after all.

Sottopassaggio

A Novel
By Nick Alexander

I don't know how I ended up in Brighton.
I'm in a permanent state of surprise about it. Of course I know the events that took place, I remember the accident or rather I remember the last time Steve ever looked into my eyes before the grinding screeching wiped it all out. It all seems so unexpected, so far from how things were supposed to be...

Following the loss of his partner, Mark, the hero from the bestselling *50 Reasons to Say, "Goodbye"*, tries to pick up the pieces and build a new life for himself in gay friendly Brighton.
Haunted by the death of his lover and a fading sense of self, Mark struggles to put the past behind him, exploring Brighton's high and low-life, falling in love with charming, but unavailable Tom, and hooking up with Jenny, a long lost girlfriend from a time when such a thing seemed possible. But Jenny has her own problems, and as all around are inexorably sucked into the violence of her life, destiny intervenes, weaving the past to the present, and the present to the future in ways no one could have imagined.

"Alexander has a beautifully turned ear for a witty phrase... I think we can all recognise the lives that live within these pages, and we share their triumphs and tragedies, hopes and lost dreams." - Joe Galliano, Gay Times

ISBN: 2-9524-8991-2

BIGfib Books.

www.BIGfib.com

Good Thing Bad Thing

A Novel
By Nick Alexander

On holiday with new boyfriend Tom, Mark - the hero from the best-selling novels, *50 Reasons to Say, "Goodbye"* and *Sottopassaggio* - heads off to rural Italy for a spot of camping.
When the ruggedly seductive Dante invites them onto his farmland the lovers think they have struck lucky, but there is more to Dante than meets the eye - much more.
Thoroughly bewitched, Tom, all innocence, appears blind to Dante's dark side... Racked with suspicion, it is Mark who notices as their holiday starts to spin slowly but very surely out of control - and it is Mark, alone, who can maybe save the day...

Good Thing, Bad Thing is a story of choices; an exploration of the relationship between understanding and forgiveness, and an investigation of the fact that life is rarely quite as bad - or as good - as it seems. Above all *Good Thing, Bad Thing* is another cracking adventure for gay everyman Mark.

"Spooky, and emotionally turbulent - yet profoundly comedic, this third novel in a captivating trilogy is a roller-coaster literary treasure all on its own. But do yourself a favour, and treat yourself to its two prequels as soon as you can..." - Richard Labonte, Book Marks

ISBN: 2-9524-8992-0

BIGfib Books.

www.BIGfib.com

Also Available From BIGfib Books

Better Than Easy

A Novel by Nick Alexander

We know that we will die, yet we somehow manage not to think about it, and we do this because it's the only way to live; the only sensible choice is to believe naively that happiness is here, that this relationship is the right one and that we will all live happily ever after. It's perhaps revealing that believe and naïve should rhyme so well...

Better Than Easy – the fourth volume in the bestselling 50 Reasons series – finds Mark about to embark on the project of a lifetime, the purchase of a hilltop gîte in a remote French village with partner Tom.
But with shady dealings making the purchase unexpectedly complex, Mark finds himself with time on his hands – time to consider not only if this is the right project but whether Tom is the right man.
A chance meeting with a seductive Latino promises nirvana yet threatens to destroy every other relationship Mark holds dear, and as he navigates a seemingly endless ocean of untruths, Mark is forced to question whether any worthwhile destination remains.
Better Than Easy combines a tense tale of betrayal and a warming exploration of the mix of courage and naivety required if we are to choose love and happiness – if we are to continue to believe against seemingly impossible odds.

"Alexander asks and answers questions central to the homo condition in this perceptive, entertaining novel that showcases his warm wit, his wry insight, and his commendable knack for crafting queer characters with real dimension. Gay fiction doesn't get much better." – Books to Watch Out For

"*Better Than Easy* is my favourite of Nick Alexander's novels so far. It's sweet, sexy, funny and tender, and I'm not ashamed to say I laughed and cried." – Paul Burston, Time Out London.

ISBN: 2-9524899-7-1
www.BIGfib.com

13:55 Eastern Standard Time

A Novel by Nick Alexander

Alice looks at the phone and then glances at the alarm clock. 13:55 pm EST makes - she counts on her fingers - about six p.m. in Berlin. He'll be on his way home. Alice settles into the armchair and dials the number...

If Alice hadn't bumped into Will then she would probably never have phoned that afternoon. And if Alice hadn't called then Michael, poor Michael, might still be alive today...

"Both short story collection and novel, *13:55 Eastern Standard Time* finds Nick Alexander at his best. Sometimes disturbing, sometimes funny, these are stories of lives that cross and collide in life-ending drama, or simply run peacefully alongside for a few hours - lives filled with characters who are attracted and repelled, hopeless and yet inspired.
Narrated in Alexander's trademark tense prose, these interwoven stories explore the ripples emanating from our every act, ripples that alter distant destinies, and occasionally bounce back, catching us from behind to haunt or inspire.
13:55 Eastern Standard Time repeats the success of Alexander's first novel, *50 Reasons to Say, "Goodbye"* because again, as with life itself, the whole is mysteriously greater than the sum of the parts."

"...the overall effect is dazzling. Nick Alexander has reinvented Gay fiction... *13:55 Eastern Standard Time* is a novel, a collection of short stories, and a whole lot more besides." – Time Out, June '07

ISBN: 2-9524899-6-3

www.BIGfib.com

Lightning Source UK Ltd.
Milton Keynes UK
21 February 2011

167908UK00002B/284/P